THE FULL CIRCLE

THE FULL CIRCLE

HAIG TAHTA

BLACK
APOLLO
PRESS

First published in Great Britain by
Black Apollo Press, 2013

ISBN: 9781900355803

A CIP catalogue record of this book is available at
the British Library.

For information regarding our other titles, please go
to our website:
www.blackapollo.com

Chapter 1

CONRAD

I suppose that the one universal experience about being in prison, wherever you are and whatever the circumstances, is how all at once you have the time to reflect on your past. Not only perhaps to think about the very circumstances that have put you into this quandary in the first place, but also on the whole of your past life. I toyed with this thought whilst I sat in a small cell in Brixton Prison waiting for my son to make the necessary arrangements to bail me out. It was the millennium year – the celebrations were over, and I was seventy-seven years old, and feeling every bit of it. But then it struck me as to how arrogant and western-oriented this thought was. This 'time for reflection' that has been granted when you find yourself in prison is really only possible where you are reasonably comfortable, know that you are going to be fed and fairly certain that you are not going to be tortured. Primo Levi, incarcerated in Auschwitz, made it clear enough in his book "Is this a man" that the only thoughts he was capable of during his time in prison were how to keep warm, where the next meal was coming from and how to avoid the next brutal beating.

I confess that I had no such fears that I would suffer in any similar way from the generally cheerful and well-intentioned prison guards that I had encountered so far in Brixton. However, I have been familiar with imprisonment of one kind or another in my past. My recent experience of the violent – yes, I could certainly call it violent – death of a loved one, the direct cause of my present confinement in one of H.M's prisons, drove my mind back for the first time for many years to the violent death of my young brother, almost fifty years ago.

Ah! Billy - my naïve, trusting, younger brother, always madly in love with someone, always looking to me in complete, self-centred confidence to relieve him from all the difficulties that he ever encountered in his short life! At the end, bruised and beaten almost to the point of death, he had lain by the side of that road in Malaya, lying in my arms, dying; and for the first time in our lives I could not help him. In his last moments he had looked up and recognised me. He had shown no surprise at all, though the circumstances were such that he could not have explained to himself how I came to be there at that moment. His eyes had then lit up with a joy that, even in the desperate situation we were both in, gave me a real moment of happiness – ecstasy even – a joy that I have never experienced in quite the same way since. He mumbled something, which, in the noise of all the shooting going on around us, I did not hear all that clearly. It was something on the lines of "Again brother – you've come to save me again, brother." He said it in Armenian – a language we rarely used together, though we were both half Armenian. I don't know why he chose to say it in that language – possibly because I was cradling him in my arms saying "Yeghpirus, Yeghpirus"(my brother, my brother) over and over again willing him to recover consciousness. Then the mumbling faded away, the light .in his eyes dimmed and I saw that he was dead.

My political superior and certainly by then my friend, Sir Henry Gurney the High Commissioner of Malaya, had just died on that road right in front of my eyes – the victim of a hail of bullets, one of which had finally killed Billy and one of which had hit me as well. Everything had happened in seconds. .I was losing blood and I had no time to think. The Chinese leader of that group of communist guerrillas – Siu Mah – who had masterminded the assassination, ran out of the jungle as the shooting died down. I stood up leaving Billy still on the ground. I don't know what I was thinking – I suppose I was expecting to be shot there and then, but all I remember was that for some reason or another I was determined not to leave Billy. I watched as another twenty or thirty Chinese guerrillas ran out of the surrounding jungle at his command. I could see that both the drivers of the two cars were dead. My senses were sharpened to the point that I could even hear faintly the sound of the police car which was supposed to have been our escort, far down the mountainside now coming up the road – perhaps now only five minutes away. I was experiencing a combination of real fear together with a heightened awareness of every detail around me, mixed in with an indescribable sadness, not yet entirely accepted, of standing over the dead body of my brother. I remember standing there staring at the grim face of the Chinaman, who I suddenly thought might even be Chin Peng himself, the reputed leader of the Communist Insurgents.

Then with a gesture, Siu Mah signalled to two of his men to pick up Billy's body. also signalling me to follow them. At that point a red wave of anger washed over me as I stood over the body and I made it clear that no one was to touch him. This all happened in a few seconds. There was a moment's hesitation and then the leader, still pointing his revolver directly at me, signalled that I should myself pick up the body and come with him. This time I did not hesitate, being well aware that any alternative was death. I knelt and braced myself for the effort of lifting Billy – as I was certainly not going to let anyone else touch him.

Grief than overwhelmed me all over again as I realised how light he was – his body had not only been beaten, but he must have been deprived of food for some time before I found him. I picked up his wasted corpse. Carrying him in my arms – I could not bring myself to have his body suffer the indignity of draping it over my shoulder – I stumbled into the cool depths of the surrounding jungle. I was prodded forward urgently from behind as I heard the sound of the approaching police van. It was clear to me even then that the guerrillas did not want to leave any evidence of why the cars had stopped and what it was that had made Sir Henry get out of the car. The whole party, with me at the front immediately behind Siu Mah, melted away into the gloom of the surrounding trees and undergrowth.

A feeling of lassitude sweeps over me as my memory fades and I lean back on my cot – really perfectly comfortable compared to what most prisoners have to face – and try to remember what had happened after that dramatic moment on the 6th October 1951 - the date is seared into my brain - that went down in history as the day of the assassination of Sir Henry Gurney, the High Commissioner of Malaya. I recall that it was a turning-point in the Malayan Emergency, but what happened to me afterwards as I stumbled into the jungle? I haven't repressed it or anything, but memory is like that. Certain moments in one's past stand out with every detail sharp and clear, whilst other periods, not perhaps so immediate, have to be recalled and pieced together, episode by episode.

So it is that I can remember every detail of that day and of the days before, while I was frantically seeking to solve the problem of my abducted brother. In general and somewhat to my surprise, as I reach old age my memory of the days of my childhood and my youth and the carefree years before I got married become clearer and more vivid; whilst the long years of getting married, having children, holding down a job, raising the kids, working and playing, loving and bickering, begin to fade into one great mushy whole. Life is in any case not what you have actually lived, but only what you can recall. Furthermore what you recollect may itself be false as a result of the way in which you create a narrative of your experiences almost from the first moment.

So whilst the memory of that day remains fixed and fresh in my memory, the interminable days of pain, grief and some fear that followed are lost in a grey mist. I remember carrying Billy in my arms on that first day staggering along tracks through the jungle, with vines and twigs and bushes scratching my face and arms as I stumbled on in a mix of tears and impotent anger. Although Siu Mah, the Marxist leader that I came to know so well in the next weeks, could not have known then that the body in my arms was my brother, both he and the grim dedicated Chinese communists he led clearly had some deference for what to them must have seemed my extraordinary grief for an unknown British soldier. I have to say that I was not badly treated on that first day, apart from the prodding in my back whenever I faltered, nor in fairness in the days that followed of creeping as their prisoner through the jungle.

That first evening after we had trekked for about four hours we stopped in a little clearing through which ran an attractive small stream. It was here that Billy was buried. Siu Mah, who spoke fairly good English and who as soon as we stopped learnt of my relationship to the dead soldier, motioned four of his men to dig a grave. They all then stood aside as I lay Billy down. They waited as I stood by the side of the grave and mumbled the Lords Prayer. Poor Billy – not a believer at all, he thought that if there was a God He resided in the Laws of Physics – but I always was more conventional than the rest of my family and I could not think of anything else to say. One of the guerrillas, he didn't look more than 16 years old, came up to me and offered me a little wooden cross that he had prepared. I stood irresolute for a moment, but then thanked him as deeply as I could show, but I waved it aside. I have always been a bit conventional and diffident about my own religious feelings – but I did know that Billy was never at all confused. He was not only emphatically not a Christian, but had totally imbibed his grandfather's logical positivism and anti-clericalism. Instead therefore, I placed two large flattish stones at the head of the grave in an attempt to mark the spot in some way. I stood in the greying dusk staring at the grave as it was filled in. I was surprised to see about ten of these dedicated and grimly serious unsentimental Marxist terrorists one by one pick a large stone and lay it by the side of and on top of my two and then walk away to where they were preparing their overnight camp. I suppose, now that I think about it again, that Siu Mah must have told them that the dead British soldier was my brother.

My memory fades. Did I spend the whole night staring down at that mound? Did any of these young men join me at any point? I no longer know. The next weeks passed in a whirl of movement and daily danger and I no longer kept any record in my mind of each day's events.

Many many years later I made a major effort to find Billy's tomb. It should surely not have been difficult. I took a holiday with all my family to Singapore, and we drove up and stayed at a hotel in the much-changed hill resort of Frasers Hill, which I had never reached on that ill-fated day. On the second day, leaving my wife

Harriet and my three younger children, I went with my eldest son, William, taking back-packs – and we trekked down to the well- marked spot where Gurney was assassinated. We intended to spend one night out. William was only 14, but he was fit and was as eager as I was to try and find the spot where his only Uncle, if he had lived, lay buried. After all he knew that he was named after this unknown Uncle. Like Billy himself I had a good sense of direction and as we set off into the jungle at the same spot that I recalled, I was sure we would have no difficulty. But try as we might, searching for two days, we never found the spot. Billy's last resting place was gone forever.

All these thoughts now reminded me of William himself. Where had he got to? He was an experienced solicitor for heaven's sake, the senior partner of a small but efficient firm specialising in criminal law. He should have sorted out my bail position by now. After all, although death was the reason for the charges that had been laid against me, I was not actually accused of murder or anything quite like that and I had been assured that bail should not cause any difficulty. I calmed myself and settled back. With my mind still on those weeks in the fifties I tried to focus on what had happened in those days and weeks after Billy was buried.

It was clear both to Siu Mah himself and to all his men that the British authorities were now making a supreme effort to smoke out the gang that had successfully assassinated the most important Imperial Officer in Malaya. The British soldiers patrolling the jungles of Malaya may all have been citizen-conscripts and not regulars, but they were effective in a way that all the aircraft, helicopters, and sophisticated weaponry of another power operating in Vietnam next door, never were. Within a week of the assassination we all knew as we stumbled our way through the jungle that we were being hunted. I talked freely with Siu Mah in the evenings when we camped for the night. At first I thought that all our moving around was arbitrary, but then I recognised a pattern of avoidance. It was a period of thunderstorms and violent rain and Siu Mah split us into smaller and smaller groups and ordered everyone to move in circles to confuse the mostly Malay trackers employed by the British patrols. Ah! – this reminds me that not one of this particular group of guerrillas who were my captors was a Malay – they were all Chinese.

There were at least a couple of short violent engagements between one or two of the now separate groups trying to escape the tightening British ring and the patrols, but not one in which the small group led by Siu Mah of which I was now the prisoner was involved. Siu Mah told me that he had already lost six men. He clearly enjoyed sitting with me in the evenings giving me his life history and expounding on Marxist theory, and explaining what was going to happen when the British were forced to leave. I have always had this capacity to listen to people and to persuade them to open to me their thoughts and motivations. To this day I cannot tell how or why I managed to stay alive. None of these CTs were soft or in any way sentimental. My hands were always manacled though I was no longer forced to have them behind my back. At the time I was thinking only of how to stay alive on a day-by-day basis, but now that I sit back and think about it again, I can still not come to any certain conclusion as to why I survived. Clearly Siu Mah had some idea of using me for something, perhaps as some sort of hostage, and that's why he kept dragging me along. A shot in the back of the head would have been so easy at any time – but it never came.

It was about nine weeks after the day of the assassination that the group I was travelling with – Siu Mah and seven others – was caught crossing an open clearing by a British patrol which had been waiting in an ambush position in the jungle to the side. For once the CT guerrillas, experts in ambush themselves, were caught in an ambush laid by a clever Malay tracker and the Chinese interpreter to this particular British patrol. I was in the middle of the line of seven men, Siu Mah was right at the front. He had just reached the first line of trees on the other side of the clearing, at the moment that the last man in our line came out from the trees on our side, when a fusillade of shots rang out. I was in the middle right in the open. Siu Mah himself and the first four men ran on into the jungle and turned to shoot back into the jungle from where the shots were coming. The man behind me was shot and died instantly. I too felt a bullet graze my shoulder. Without a moment's thought I fell to the ground and tried to make myself as small as possible. The last two men in the line, without Siu Mah's leadership, rather foolishly did not race back into the trees but knelt and returned fire – but as they couldn't see the enemy, they too were soon killed. Firing from the front soon stopped as Siu Mah and his men slipped away into the jungle.

There was now an ominous silence as the British patrol came ever so carefully and gingerly out, all with their fingers on their triggers; ready to shoot at a moment's notice. At that moment I felt more in danger from this patrol than in all the weeks of stumbling around with those grim Chinese guerrillas. I managed to raise my hands up into the air in a traditional gesture of surrender – but also in the hope that someone would see the manacles.

I was lucky. No one shot and I was soon in the hands of a cheerful group of teenagers – for that's all they were, all National Service men – led by a couple of grizzled regular Sergeants and one surprised officer. Now once again my memory fades again and I remember little of what transpired before I got back to an Army base. Before I was flown back to England, however, I had to go through a de-briefing process in Kuala Lumpur. It was singularly inefficient. I had after all myself been an Intelligence Officer with the army for seven years, and I sat in surprise as the interrogation continued. He was an arrogant public school type. He never once touched on the reasons that I was found as a prisoner with that particular group of insurgents. I never volunteered any information about the assassination and he never asked. By the time of the interrogation I was already aware of the widespread belief that Gurney had got out of the relative safety of the car in order to draw any fire away from Lady Gurney. I had always admired Gurney and I did not want to muddy the waters by disclosing the contribution provided by the unfortunate Billy. What good could it do? The interrogating officer made a hopeless task of it, but he did make one sensible suggestion when I asked if he could satisfy a point which had been puzzling me over the weeks – namely why I had been allowed to survive for so long. 'Ah', he said. 'whoever the guy was who captured you, he wanted to produce you before Chin Peng for him to interrogate, and also to show him how bright and efficient he was –it would be counted as a step up for him.'

Could be – could be!

He really was in all other respects an example of the worst kind of haughty and amateur Imperial officer. Keeping what had occurred on that day all to myself at that de-briefing then became a habit to me later as the events faded and passed into history. I had already telegraphed my parents before the assassination telling them that Billy had been abducted by the terrorists and shot – and this was how the record stayed. I never told the truth to Olga my mother. However, sitting alongside my father, Harry, in the hospital where he died, I held his hand – he remained as sharp as a button right to the very end – and told him what had happened to his only son.

Thoughts of my Dad's death and those last hours in the hospital always brought tears to my eyes. Not really grief – we all know in our hearts that our fathers must die – but the recollection of all the good times we had had together brings tears. I sat up on the bed and was just about to start a bit of a wallow nostalgically about the past, when at last the cell door opened, and a cheerful guard stood by the door and said –

"Come along, sir, your son has at last turned up and you're out on bail."

I stopped all my reminiscing about the past, which was about to turn a bit sentimental, and strode out. Good heavens, who am I fooling, the reality is that, exhausted as I was, I shuffled out.

Chapter 2

Conrad

In my present predicament facing serious criminal charges, it seems to be my relationship over the years with my wife which is so exercising the mind of the Crown Prosecution Service. I first met Harriet after the War – ah! yes of course, these days I have to specify which war I suppose. I refer to World War II. Why II? Was the Great War of 1914 really a world war? If the Ottomans had not fatally entered that war three months after it had started, it would have remained almost entirely fought in Europe; and even after the Ottomans did join in, it was still largely fought either in Europe, Gallipoli comes to mind, or very close to it. I digress – something that is happening to me a lot as I get older. I was always prone to it, but somehow nowadays as I talk about a subject I find that a word or a thought will turn me onto another subject before I have really finished with the original.

I had been an Intelligence officer with the army during that war. After the war ended I went on to work for the British military authority in Palestine until the very month before the Mandate was relinquished and the State of Israel declared. I then took up my place as a student at Oxford, a place that I had first been granted seven years before.

Harriet, my feisty beautiful Harriet, attracted me from the first moment that I met her during what was for both of us our first term. She was at Somerville, a college close to mine – Worcester. We shared the same tutor in late medieval and early Renaissance Italian literature. Dante of course. Where were that tutor's rooms?. Somewhere in or near Wadham I think. I invited her to have a coffee with me after that first tutorial, and we began seeing each other fairly regularly after that. Quite apart from the mutual attraction, my Italian was completely fluent after years of interrogating Italian prisoners of war, and I was able to help her with tricky points in the texts.

This was the Autumn term of 1948, an extraordinary period in the premier University of England when the student population was comprised on the one side of prematurely matured young men over 25 who had just gone through 5 or 6 years of war fought all over Europe and the Far East; and on the other side a somewhat lesser number of precocious, clever but immature youngsters straight from school. The mixture was tense, indeed almost explosive, but very stimulating. I remember it all as having an almost ascetic monastic quality, save that in the midst of all that serious discussion about socialism, religion and philosophy there was also a lot of sex, with both the teenagers discovering themselves on the one hand and all those jaded warriors on the other. The great sexual revolution of the sixties was still ten years away, but already there were many more girls at the University than before – and there was of course as always the lovely compliant nurses of the Radcliffe.

Harriet was on the short side with long dark hair that came down to the middle of her back when she combed it out. Her eyes were a very dark blue, which turned almost black when she was aroused or angry. Our coffee mornings once a week after our joint tutorial were a joy to me. Our discussions ranged over a vast area, and I was overwhelmed by the breadth of her interests and her understanding. Then came the day she asked if I could help her with a piece of translation set by her language and grammar tutor. I had rooms in the main buildings on the right as you enter the Worcester College Quad and I arranged that she was to come the next day in the afternoon. She did. I can no longer recall exactly the many times that she came after that, but it was certainly more than once a week.

Look I must be clear – life has changed so much since then that I have to spell it out. This was not yet even the fifties, never mind what became the norm ten years later. Casual sex was not normal. Quite apart from the tenor of the times, I respected her mind and personality to the point that I could not at that stage indulge in the stirrings in my groin of which I occasionally became uncomfortably aware. She was only 18 or perhaps 19 – certainly still a teenager, even though sometimes she could act as if she was much older. I recall that in that first term we did all the usual things that students at Oxford did then – the new coffee shops – punting on the river – picnics – meetings with friends in pubs.

Then in the next term, Harriet met the man who lived on the same staircase opposite me. Jake Astley was my age. He too had been through the war, and he too like me was taking up the place he had been offered in 1940/41 before being called up. I liked Jake. He was not a subtle man. He always acted very directly and decisively and didn't think too much before he did so. But he had a fund of funny stories and he was a welcome change from all the gauche excitable 18-year olds, all just learning for the first time how to enjoy a pint of beer, who thronged around us. I was well aware that he was not only good-looking in an entirely conventional Anglo-Saxon way, but that he exuded an aggressive self-confident sexuality which was obviously attractive to some women. A descendent of that eponymous Royalist General who commanded the King's Infantry at Edgehill, he had that effortless self-confidence which was the quality of the English upper classes which I most admired – and most hated.

During this period of my life I always had difficulty in my relationship with girls of my own class and style. I was not shy. I never had the slightest difficulty in approaching and chatting to friends and even strangers of both sexes. But somehow once I came to know a girl with whom I could chat easily and whom I respected, I became inhibited in respect of any physical expression. It was as if as soon as I became aware of the personality and mind of the 'woman' behind the attractive girl, I lost the desire to impose any drive to initiate physical contact. Ridiculous really – too much empathy! From the first moment of adolescent fantasies, I have always been completely heterosexual in my feelings – unlike, I suspect, my brother Billy, who was liable to 'fall in love' with anybody at the drop of a hat. My inhibitions with Harriet during this period remain a mystery to me even now. It was not as if I was at the same stage as all the young men around me. I had already experienced a strong physical relationship with a young girl during the time I was stationed in Palestine only the year or two before – though that was one of those rare occasions when the physical contact arose before we had any real knowledge of each other. If I had got to know her well before we got to bed together, my inhibitions being what they are, it might never have happened.

In the end Harriet, after meeting and getting to know Jake, fell for his somewhat aggressive charm.. Harriet's arrival in the afternoons onto our staircase now ended up in Jake's rooms rather than mine. Furthermore the 'oak' would be sported most of the afternoon leaving little doubt as to what was going on. In the course of the recent police and other interrogations that I have been going through, I have been questioned particularly on this period. I have not been believed when I have asserted and still do assert that I was not jealous at the time – and never have been. Jealousy is not an emotion – or should I say vice – that I recognise in myself. I was never, for instance, jealous at the time of the birth of my younger siblings. So, whilst I was sorry that this fascinating woman had fallen for someone who was not in my opinion worthy of her, I was not jealous. I liked Jake, he was good company, but in the last resort he was a right-wing jerk who had no idea at all of any woman's real worth. I suppose this might sound a bit like reflected jealousy, but I'm sure it isn't.

Harriet kept on seeing me despite the afternoons with Jake, and we had no problem in resuming our coffee breaks and our exploration of each other's ideas. She was always very open about her relationship with Jake and I was led to believe by her that they were engaged – or at least all but. However, when I mentioned this once to Jake he just laughed and made no comment, and I got the impression that he thought the whole idea was a good joke. That summer I went to Florence and stayed for three months with my Aunt and her sisters. I had previously met them in 1944 when I was attached to the Eighth Army as it struggled its way up the Italian peninsula and liberated the city. Meanwhile during that same summer Harriet had taken herself off on a road trip somewhere in the Middle East in the company of yet another young man.

It all begins to get a bit muddled in my memory, but during the following term, Harriet continued to float back regularly into the arms of Jake – but this term I sensed a tension in her whenever we sat together and talked. The following summer we all went to Florence again - that is Billy came as well as Harriet and I. Billy was I suppose 17 then. His excitable enthusiasms got on Harriet's nerves I think and she often teased him – quite cruelly sometimes. He didn't seem to mind, and meanwhile my relations with Harriet deepened. Billy was a good lad and he kept out of our way during those summer months. I knew then that I was falling in love – perhaps for the first time in my life – with this exciting woman. By now too it was becoming obvious to me that Harriet was either no longer in thrall to Astley – or in truth never had been.

We all went to Siena one day to watch the annual Palio event. After we returned to Florence, Billy, for some reason that I have never ever understood, decided to go home to do his National Service, which in view of his brilliant Mathematics scholarship he could easily have deferred. Somehow that trip to Siena changed everything and all the inhibitions that I had had melted away, and within a few days of Siena - I don't remember exactly when –Harriet and I consummated our love in a shady spot on the banks of the Arno.

Several matters then arose after we returned to England. First I had to finish University. Then I had to get a job. This was much easier in those days than it seems to be now. In the end after trying out one or two different options I became a journalist specialising in foreign affairs. My fluency in so many languages was a great benefit to me in this field and I was successful in getting many of the plum postings for my newspaper. Then came the trauma of the death of Billy on the road up to Frasers Hill which I have already described. But I had already made up my mind even while still in Malaya that when I got home I would ask Harriet to marry so we could set up home together.

It wasn't quite as easy as I had envisaged. For a start I had to face up to the unfortunate fact that my mother – Olga – never liked Harriet much. I never quite knew why and I put it down to the old problem of wives and mothers-in-law. It had something to do with some insight or feminine instinct that Mum had about Billy – but I never knew why. Harriet always tried her best, but there it was and I had to take it into account. There is no way that I have the capacity to ride rough-shod over the feelings of people I love. But I persevered and won through.

We were married in a Registry Office in Purley near my parent's house. My sister and my parents were there of course, and Harriet's rather grim mother Tessa came down from Manchester. My Dad took everyone out after the ceremony to a fabulous Hotel, whose name or situation I cannot now remember – it certainly wasn't in Purley. My eldest son William was born about two years later.

Chapter 3

Charles

I was not quite sure at the time why I had been chosen to be the one to carry out our investigations further into the case of R. v. Bridgeman, which was coming to a boil during that millennium year of 2000. I was unmarried and one of the youngest of the members of the special committee of the Crown Prosecution Service (the CPS) – a committee which had been formed to consider the Bridgeman case. My colleagues on that committee were all married men, and all older than me. I decided at first that my bachelor status must have been the deciding factor, but I was wrong. Before taking my law degree I had studied Psychology at University, and it turned out that the committee thought that my BA in that subject would save them from having to instruct an outside expert to report on any psychological aspect of the case, which would have been the normal procedure.

In the situation facing the CPS in this case, one of the factors which had to be considered by the committee, probably the most important one, was the relationship – past and present – of Conrad Bridgeman with his wife which was central to the whole question that we had to evaluate. It was this relationship that I was instructed to investigate as soon as possible after Bridgeman was released from Brixton on bail.

Bridgeman had left the army in 1948 as an Acting Major, after a distinguished career during the war as an Intelligence Officer. I discovered that he had worked for the Army from 1941 when he was first called up, as an Officer attached to the Eighth Army in Libya involved in the interrogation of Italian prisoners-of-war. His linguistic skills and the ability he seemed to have of getting information out of people, meant that towards the end he was the officer dealing with the most senior of the captured enemy officers. The Army needed him and he was not immediately demobilised at the end of the war but went for a two years posting to Trieste, which was, it seems, at the time a critical spot in the developing cold war in post-war Europe. From here he was posted to Palestine, where he worked for the Mandate authority for about a year, being demobilised in April 1948 just before the Mandate was finally relinquished.

Bridgeman gave clear notice both to the Police and to the CPS that he would be returning to England early in the new year – that would be in March 2000. It was suggested by the Chairman of the special committee which had been set up by the CPS that I should start my side of the investigation by being present in Dover when he arrived and was arrested. I duly drove down to Dover and was in the Arrivals building about half an hour before the Car Ferry, which Bridgeman had boarded in Calais, was due in. The Chief Inspector dealing with the case was there with two uniformed men, although of course no trouble of any kind was anticipated. Bridgeman's son, William, was also there, in his capacity both as his eldest child, but also in his capacity as the man's Solicitor. I tried to get out of him what line he would be taking in the defence, but he was unwilling to talk and frankly I got nowhere, though he did not snub me in any way and was tolerant as I talked generally about his father and mother.

As this was a case where the other family members were also material to the prosecution, I should report that in my conversation with him I sensed no hesitation or any over-emotional commitment emanating from him. He was cool and appeared detached and highly professional in his demeanour towards me and towards the Chief Inspector. He accepted that his father was to be arrested as soon as his car came off the ferry and drove into the terminal. The plan was that the car would be shunted off into a side section by the Customs officers on duty, where Bridgeman would then be arrested. The arrangement agreed was that after his arrest, his son, William, who had come down to Dover by train, would collect the car once his father had been led off and drive it back home.

Whereas my first reaction to William Bridgeman was that he was a cool, decisive and unemotional young man, the first meeting between him and his father quickly disabused me of that impression. Major Bridgeman was in his seventies, and William was, as I ascertained later, only just in his forties – but there was no question of handshakes or formal embraces. As Conrad Bridgeman got somewhat wearily out of the car, his son was onto him in a second. Their love and embrace was total and without any Anglo-Saxon reserve of any kind – none of that back-slapping that English and American males indulge in to cover the basic lack of comfort that they feel when embracing another man, however close the relationship. I was reminded that Bridgeman was half-Armenian – and by all accounts it was an important half.

I will have to report that the arrest went off without any difficulty whatsoever. Once he was released from the fierce embrace of his son, Bridgeman shook hands with everyone and was driven away in the Police Van. There were no reporters, the whole matter not as yet having moved into the public domain. I believe that it was about two days later – or even on the very next day, that Major Bridgeman was released on bail and returned to his house – the old matrimonial home in Purley where he was currently living with his youngest daughter.

I had introduced myself – Charles Tierney – to the man when he came forward politely to shake hands. At that moment I had asked him if I might call and interview him after, of course, he had given his formal statement to the Police. Needless to say his son William had immediately intervened there and then, making it clear that he would not agree to any such meeting of any kind. "Disgraceful" – "Completely outrageous proposal" was the mildest epithets that he hurled at me in that Customs Shed. He was very angry and shouted that if I insisted I could "jolly well go and get a Judge to make an order allowing the interview, but that he would fight it all the way. Well to be honest I sort of agreed with him – but then his father intervened. He smiled and suggested that I telephone him once he got home. All of us were quite aware that in the circumstances bail was likely to be only a formality.

I arranged my first meeting with Conrad some days after he got out of Brixton. Yes, certainly, my using that personal name is deliberate - for after that first meeting he was no longer Bridgeman of R.v.Bridgeman for me. He had entirely overruled his own son and agreed to talk to me on condition that everything said between us was to be 'off the record' so far as any later trial was concerned, though he agreed that I could of course report the interview to the CPS committee of which I was a part. His son wrote a very sharp letter to the CPS making clear his attitude as Conrad's solicitor. I believe he took it even further and sent a copy of the letter to the Law Society. In the end, while I understand that the Law Society too was not happy, Conrad's own decision, against his solicitor's advice, to allow a private interview could not be overruled. Heaven knows what yelling and shouting went on between William and his father – but whatever went on between them, the interview went forward.

During this first interview which went on for about three hours, Conrad's youngest daughter – Sima – came in and out a couple of times with coffee and bits and pieces. She was in her early thirties, or even late twenties - I couldn't tell. Unlike her brother William, the solicitor, she had very Armenian features, which sort of suited her name. I accept that I really have no idea what constitutes 'Armenian features', but I know myself what I meant. Conrad's youngest son – Nicholas, usually referred to as Nikko, also once made a somewhat rumbustious entrance. Neither of the two was subdued or appeared to be in any emotional turmoil – at least none that I could ascertain. On every one of the occasions that I interviewed Conrad at his home I always ended up being invited to stay for lunch, which on that first occasion I accepted rather diffidently, but which on every later occasion I accepted with alacrity and great pleasure.

Conrad was very open and frank throughout each of my interviews. We discussed at length how he had met Harriet during his University days. He referred to Harriet's first liaison with a mutual friend, Jake – still alive and now Sir Jacob Astley – and how they had consummated what must have been Harriet's first love affair. I could trace no sense of betrayal or feelings of jealousy when Conrad talked to me of this relationship. However I might be wrong – it is possible that throughout his life Conrad has had resentments buried deep inside him and which he has refused to confront.

For ten years the marriage seems to have progressed in a fairly normal way. William was born in 1958 and the eldest daughter Anne the year after. There was then a gap of nine years before the birth of Sima, and a year later Nikko. During the sixties Conrad got his permanent job as foreign correspondent for a major national daily which took him away for long periods.. It was during this period in the late sixties that Conrad finally admitted to me, during our second interview, that he believed – no that he knew – that Harriet had had a fairly intense affair with a neighbour. The neighbour in question was a wealthy Greek shipping magnate, who was not only a business man controlling a small fleet of freighters, but was actually a Ship's Captain himself with all the necessary licences and qualifications to act directly as a Ship's Master.

I pressed Conrad on this subject. He was at first loath to talk much about it, continuing always to aver that jealousy was not in his nature and that this was an emotion he had never experienced. My own thought was that "methinks he doth protest too much". Surely no man can feel comfortable at the thought of his wife coupling with another man. Every man of any sensitivity at all has that slight anxiety as to how his wife relates to their sexual union, and as to how she would compare his way of making love to that of another man – particularly, I would have thought, in the case of such a sexual bombshell, as I soon realised that Harriet Bridgeman had been. It is that anxiety about how you compare in the sexual act which is the core of the problem for the male – not the anxiety about the passing on of genes that is the current mantra from the biologists. As I probed further, it became clear that he had been away quite a lot in the period before the birth of Nikko.

Conrad eventually confessed to me that before her untimely death Harriet had admitted to him that she had indeed had a fully consummated affair with this Stavros guy which had gone on for almost two whole years. Conrad claimed that at no time did he ask her whether Nikko was his biological son, nor did they ever discuss it together. I have to say that I did not believe him and I still don't. Conrad may or may not be that rare man who has no element of jealousy in his relations with his wife or indeed with others – but I cannot believe that in the dramatic circumstances of this last year he did not explore with her the possibility of any doubt as to the paternity of that young man. I do accept, however, that it is also possible that as between he and I this was a personal step too far – and that he would not discuss the paternity of one of his children with me, even if he was prepared to go fairly frankly into the affairs of his deceased wife.

I will go on to say, however, that when I come to write my report I will be taking the view that Harriet's deep but fickle sexuality, and her several affairs with several different men, did not affect the actions of Conrad Bridgeman during this last year in respect of the matters we are investigating.

I cannot believe Conrad's assertions that he was never affected by the certain knowledge that came to him during this last year about Harriet's infidelities. Neither can I accept that he has no jealousy in his make-up. That may be what he thinks about his own character, but if I was to analyse it in depth, I would suggest that he has repressed it for all these years. Nevertheless, despite all that, I must stick to my view that none of this has affected his recent actions.

Chapter 4

Sima

Neither I nor Nikko had taken any great part in the long and interminable discussions which had taken place within the family before my father and mother left home at the beginning of that year, after all the millennium celebrations had finally ended. I wonder if anyone now remembers all that fuss there had been at that time about the computers all crashing because of the "00" situation. One of the great non-events of the whole millennium!

When my father returned from Europe and was released from Brixton I got back to my own task of looking after the house, which Harriet had impressed on me before my parents left. Frankly I am not fond of cooking, so that this chore was more often than not dealt with by Nikko who certainly fancies himself as a great cook. Good luck to him. Of course we had a cleaning lady who also did some midday cooking – but it was always Nikko who cooked for us in the evenings when he got back from work – or what he called work, though none of the rest of us would have called it that.

It was I who opened the door to Charles Tierney on that first day that he arrived to interview baba. He wasn't much older than me and he had the most frank and open expression of any man I had ever met. He was not wearing a suit, but he did have a tie and somehow he looked formal despite the casual wear. Fair brown hair a bit muffed up and not well combed, and blue eyes, he gave me a wide really kind smile and extended his hand saying "Charles Tierney ma'am – I have an interview arranged with Mr. Bridgeman." I melted. I mean I do accept that that is a fairly clichéd expression, but I really did feel myself go all soft and wobbly at the knees. But I do tend to get all sensual at first impressions of young men who I could fancy – I must get it from my mother - Harriet. But that was, as always, just a first physical reaction. It didn't last long – the basic requirements of hospitality immediately reasserted itself and I shook his hand and took him through to baba's study.

They were in there for about three or four hours on that first occasion. Whenever I went in – I suppose it was about twice – to bring them coffee and stuff, I could see that baba was under some stress. He was always superb at being able to hide his feelings, so the young man interviewing him clearly had no idea that he was causing strain to the elderly man he was interrogating. But I could see it and any fanciful thought that I had entertained for this interloper disappeared as fast as it had first appeared. How dare he harass my father in this way when he was after all already in such a turmoil of emotion as a result of what had occurred.

However, I also knew that Baba would have insisted not only on my inviting the young man to lunch, but also that I should myself always maintain the require-ments of warm hospitality towards him regardless of any feelings I might have. Accordingly I duly made the necessary arrangements and went in at 1.00 to tell them that lunch was ready. Over lunch Baba was at his most open-hearted and expansive, telling stories about his past and clearly determined to put Charles at his ease. But I knew – or at least thought I knew – that grief and guilt were now working in him and that there was a clear element of brittle hysteria in his over-enthusiastic conversation.

By mutual consent not a word was said during that lunch with regard to the situation in which baba found himself, and which Charles was supposedly investigating. I myself always took a purely practical attitude to the problem that had been so exercising the males in our family to such an excessive degree during the last six months. I was not prepared myself to indulge in the emotional overdrive that Harriet had caused to all the men in the family – my brothers and my father.

Harriet had never taken much notice of me. I think she simply didn't like me very much. Nothing overt – I mean she always did whatever was strictly required as a mother but well.... the attention that she paid towards her children – such as it was – was entirely centred round her two sons. William was from the start a forceful character and once he became an adult he was one of the few people in her family to whom she listened and whose opinion she sought and accepted. Nikko was her baby and could do no wrong, either as a child or when he grew up. My older sister Anne on the other hand grew up quickly and Harriet had accepted her as a sort of equal to whom she could unburden herself on a woman to woman basis as soon as she had grown up a little. I was not jealous of all this, or I don't think so, but I only knew that I myself did not receive any love from her, only maternal duty.

I was a bit of a late developer. Although I became physically nubile in the usual way when I was 14 or perhaps 15 – I can't now remember exactly – I did not experience any great sexual feelings then. Sex was in the air and I giggled and talked about it with all my school friends of course – but without any real physical feel of what it was all about. I don't want to mislead – this was after all the early eighties and I knew perfectly well all the facts of life, it was just that I didn't feel it down there. Nikko was then I suppose 13 or 14 years old and I know that he was quite different. Even at that age he had Harriet's deep sensuous nature. He was dark and good-looking and all my girl friends were attracted to him. He himself teased them and was teased back. For me at that time I was unaware of the latent sexual aspect to it all; nor did I ever realise that when Nikko sometimes wrestled with me in play, and we cuddled together that it was a very different experience for him to what I thought of as only just fun and affection.

In the end it all changed for me one day when I returned from school unusually early. I can't remember why – all I can be sure of was that I was over 16, as I recollect that I had just had my sixteenth birthday some weeks before. Baba had flown back specially from some god-forsaken corner of Africa where he had been covering some civil war or another. I loved that party; many of my girlfriends were there, and all my own family in full cry; mother was at her most gracious; William was just about to get married and he came with his fiancée; Baba flew in especially – I felt so proud and special as he had to leave to go back the very next day. So I am quite sure that I was over sixteen. It was about a month after that party that I returned home at about 2.00 in the afternoon – I think the school had had to be closed due to a gas leak or something equally banal and unimportant. I let myself in. I suppose I was not making much noise – I have never in fact been a very boisterous or noisy person like Nikko. People are always bound to be aware of Nikko's comings and goings, but with me it was different.

Putting down my coat and backpack in the hall, I began to go up the stairs to my own room, but before I had my feet on the first step I heard a sort of shuffling and panting noise coming from the sitting room. I had no idea what it might be, I didn't expect anyone to be in the house at that time in the day. I was – and indeed still am – a bit timid about things like mice or rats even dogs or other animals. I really didn't want to have to confront some animal that had got into the house from the garden. On the other hand I was in that state of anxiety where I needed to know one way or another what it might be. It was touch and go what I would do, as my mind then went back to a horror story about urban foxes that some girl at school had told me. In the end I knew that I couldn't go up to my room not knowing what was in the sitting room. I went over and quietly opened the door ready to shut it with a bang if it turned out to be a fox.

I stood transfixed. Harriet was on the floor on our beautiful Turkish carpet in front of the fireplace, her naked legs up in the air entwined round the back of a man who seemed to me to be fully clothed and with his trousers still on. Could that have been possible? Trousers or not, the movements he was making and the moans I heard coming from Harriet made it quite clear even to my then innocent eyes what was going on. I should I suppose have immediately turned away and crept upstairs. But somehow the fact that the woman on the floor was my own mother was not in my consciousness. She was just a woman – furthermore a sexy attractive woman. My groin stirred – my breasts too – my whole body seemed to tingle and suddenly I think it was then that I felt for the first time what all the talk and the giggling was all about. I don't know how long I stood and stared – it really could not have been very long, but it seemed both then and in retrospect like an eternity. Then the storm broke and I turned and ran upstairs and got as much relief as I could by throwing myself on my bed.

I don't know if Harriet ever knew what I had seen. I don't suppose she would have cared even if she had suspected. She certainly discovered that I was at home after the man had left, but nothing was ever said. I never knew who the man was – I'm sure I never ever saw him again. What I do know is that my sexuality developed quickly after that day. What I saw that day has remained as a sort of image in my mind and it is an image I cannot get rid of. I am the only one of my siblings who refers to mother as Harriet – but I believe that I used to call her Harriet from when I was thirteen, so it was nothing to do with what I saw that day. She always encouraged me to call her Harriet while at no time allowing any of the other children ever to call her anything but 'mama' or 'mum'.

As my own sexuality developed, I became aware for the first time that my mother did tend to be prone to falling for and having affairs with other men. I don't want to suggest that she was blatant or promiscuous. She was discreet and I think that in her own selfish way she did love my father. I still haven't spoken openly to my brothers or sister about all this, but I do know that when I once hinted at this possible scenario they all, without exception, made it clear that they could not credit that their mother - Mum – could ever have been unfaithful. The idea was quite ludicrous for them and I quickly backed off as I didn't want them to get hurt.

Oddly enough, although I love and admire baba to distraction, I never worried about his possible reaction to what surely must have been equally obvious to him. There was always something so solid and dependable about my father Conrad that it never crossed my mind that he might be hurt by Harriet's fickle loves. Odd – I backed off immediately when I realised that none of my siblings had any idea of Harriet's affairs, because I didn't want them to be hurt – but what about my Dad.

As it was clear that Baba was getting on quite well with

this Charles guy, and no longer seemed to be stressed by the interviews I began to change my attitude towards Charles all over again. Poor man he had to be complimentary about my hopeless cooking. Funnily enough on his third visit I found myself taking a little more effort and putting a little more thought into what I was doing in the kitchen. I then got a lot of pleasure when not only Charles but also Baba said how tasty it was.

Charles Tierney was a big man insofar as he was tall and well built, but his body sort of tapered and he had narrow hips and a cute smallish ass. Of course I never saw his legs, but I was willing to bet they were pretty shapely. He had soft brown hair which was not well combed and was a bit of a mess. Blue eyes and a snub nose gave his face a strongly boyish quality which made him look younger than he was – but I have to add that this somewhat belied the underlying strength of his character. Despite always being scrupulously polite, almost to an old-fashioned degree, I found myself deferring to his views in a way that was rare for me, as I usually like to have the last word in any discussions if I can.

At the end of the third visit as he was leaving, we were alone in the hall and he held my hand just that moment longer that makes all the difference if you know what I mean. He invited me to the Opera. During the lunch the week before, we had talked about music and found that we had some mutual loves. He's a funny man – he pretended that someone had given him these two tickets – and would I go with him. What a little fibber, I'm sure he went and bought them himself. But then I am at last learning not to be so gauche and I pretended along with him.

I had an absolutely fabulous evening!

Chapter 5

Conrad

I have found myself on the wrong side of the law on several previous occasions in my life. You really can't cover wars, civil disturbances, and disasters all over the world as a journalist without sometimes finding yourself unpopular with the authorities – whether the 'authorities' in question are the so-called legitimate ones, or the illegitimate ones like the guerrillas of Malaya. Almost my worst experience of imprisonment – worse in some ways than being a prisoner of the Chinese guerrillas – came on a visit I made to Istanbul when I was covering, for my newspaper, Turkish attitudes towards the Bosnian conflict in the nineties. I have not in any way repressed my memory of that week and all that arose from it, but I don't like dwelling on it much and it certainly has no relevance to my current situation.

Some days after William got me out of that dump in Brixton, Charles Tierney, whom I had first met on my arrival in Dover, turned up at the house at my invitation. I had had a violent – well as violent as I ever actually get – row with William some days before. He insisted that I had no reason at all to talk to this guy sent by the CPS. I have never seen him so angry – he was usually the coolest of my four children. A formal charge had of course already been made leading to my arrest in Dover, but it was clear that no final decision had yet been made by the CPS as to how or whether to proceed. So there was no Court Order and no obligation for me to speak to anyone, apart of course from my duty as a citizen to help the police in any investigation by them. I had of course already given them my full statement, and accordingly, said William, I needed to go no further.

But I myself felt it was quite unnecessary to hide behind such purely legalistic rights. William was livid, but even though I dislike upsetting people I love, I stood firm and told Tierney when he phoned that he was welcome to come and interview me.

Although William wanted me to stand on my rights and not have anything to do with this representative of the CPS, William had throughout the crisis taken the view that a society – any society, democratic or not – could only subsist and develop if all its citizens accepted and followed the rules of law properly laid down by that society. Anything else, like the right for the citizen to make his or her own decisions in matters of conscience for instance, would give rise in the long run to anarchy.

I, on the other hand, had always been deeply impressed by my father's experience of how he had acted as a naval officer – the Captain of a destroyer or something like that - while with the East Mediterranean fleet anchored in the bay of Smyrna in 1922. An enormous fire, deliberately started by the triumphant Turkish army after it had entered the city following on the complete defeat of the Greek army, was destroying the city and the living quarters of over a quarter of a million of the citizens. Most had desperately reached the quays but could go no further. My father had disobeyed orders and picked up as many survivors as he could, desperately swimming in the waters of the bay, who had jumped or had been pushed off the quays, escaping from the immense engulfing fire. My father of course had to face a court-martial and was in fact found technically guilty. No – that's a euphemism – there was nothing 'technical' about it, he was found guilty. He suffered a reprimand, lost his command and some seniority, though it did not seem to have affected his subsequent career. But he never wavered from the view that even a military officer, bound perhaps more tightly by the requirements of discipline, must in exceptional cases apply a moral judgement to his own actions. He always impressed on me that you can always face up to this sort of problem – social duty as opposed to personal morality – if you are certain within yourself that the actions for which you may be being pilloried were morally correct and necessary. I too had been a military officer, so I was completely responsive to the importance of discipline and the requirement of teamwork – but my later experiences confirmed that in the last resort my Dad was right.

So I had no hesitation in being ready to talk to Charles Tierney. I was surprised when he turned up as to how young he seemed to be. Well I am well into my seventies so I suppose most people are beginning to appear surprisingly young. I found that from the start I got on well with Charles. He did, however, have that awful habit that people trained in psychology have of always turning any question you may raise straight back at you. I mean you may say 'what does this signify?' or 'why did this happen?' or 'what did this or that mean in my past?" and they look at you with deep oh so sincere eyes and answer "Well now Conrad, what do you think – how do you explain it." However he was far too young for me to get irritated. It also helped for me to bear up to all his personal and emotional prying that he was a cheerful, sprightly, good-looking guy. Right from the start I thought that Sima approved of him, and she was quick to invite him to stay for lunch without consulting me, though on that first day she did not get over her usual gauche and abrupt manner with him.

From the start he forced me into recollections about

my past with Harriet. I had no difficulty in recounting my days at University and about Harriet's steamy relationship with Jake. I never touched on the fact that my mother Olga had never liked her much, nor that Harriet herself was always highly critical of my young brother – Billy – whom she clearly disliked. Then as our interviews advanced Charles delved deeper into how our life together had developed once we were married. I found myself becoming progressively more uncomfortable.

I loved my wife. I have always loved her even when we had rows, or had to live apart due to the circumstances of my job. I never had any doubts that in so far as she was capable of love at all – she loved me – at least for most of the time. I never quite knew for certain how far I was capable of fully satisfying her sexual demands, but that she loved me I was sure. I was well aware from the start of our relationship that she was a deeply sensuous person who needed and achieved great tenderness and satisfaction from the basic sexual act. It was after all mutual.

We were well into our life together when I had my first doubts. I had to be away sometimes for weeks at a time on the foreign assignments that my newspaper was requiring me to cover. At the particular time to which I am alluding, I had returned from a longish spell away and had found that there was something different about our love-making and our closeness, and at first I was unable to put my finger on quite what was different. As a couple we had known our neighbour Stavros and his rather timid wife for many years already by then. He was always like a great breath of fresh air whenever he blundered his way into our house for a four-way dinner. He never spoke – he shouted. His grandparents had originally come from Smyrna, and this sort of gave us something in common. My own parents were still alive when he came into our lives, and he charmed both of them with recollections of what his own parents had told him about that incredible moment of terror and drama in the dying days of the Ottoman Empire.

In our many encounters Stavros would always yell at me that I was not "Armenian at all", despite my mother being fully Armenian on all sides.

"Conrad, let's face it, you're far too English – where's your hot blood! You're just too reasonable and tolerant for your own good. Bloody cold Anglo-Saxon – your English genes are triumphing over your Armenian."

If I questioned him on what he thought 'being Armenian' meant, he would shout back something on the lines of –

"Armenians – well they're just another kind of Greek really – so look take lessons from me"

All this was bellowed out very good-naturedly and followed by a great goblet of wine or some spirit. I never minded, I really didn't – but then I began to notice the generous presents – the discreet glances – the gallant attentions. Quite suddenly it struck me that perhaps he and Harriet might be having some sort of affair during my absences.

By the time of our second interview I had eventually got round to telling Charles about these suspicions that I had had all those years ago. Inevitably he began probing as to my feelings at the time – and my feelings now as well. Did I resent it all? Had it made any difference to my feelings towards Harriet? How had I coped? I had difficulty in replying – it was after all 30 years ago and indeed I could not remember exactly how I had coped. But the psychologist in Charles immediately jumped on the hesitation and said "What have you been repressing all these years, sir?" I think what actually happened was that I simply put it to one side at the time and went on with my life. Nikko was born and soon after Stavros and his wife moved back to Athens – and there was no doubt at all that if there had indeed been an affair it had completely ended.

I became aware later that Harriet had further affairs during the next years, but none quite as intense or meaningful as her liaison with Stavros, which in a sense was what started her off. Charles might after all be a little right - if that is a possible phrase. Surely you are either right or wrong – can you really be 'a little right'? I cannot recall any details at all of what could have been any further affairs – neither the name of any man, nor the facts of any suspicion, but Stavros remains very clear in my memory. He was in any case a larger than life character, but whilst all that heavy charm and the gallantry remains in my mind. I really don't think that I was ever conventionally jealous, or that I have repressed some deep desire to cut off the man's balls or anything like that. However, it was clear enough to me that Charles simply did not believe me.

During that last trip that I made with Harriet, the subject of all this investigation, she did confirm the truth of the affair with Stavros. No mention was made of any other man, but she did admit to having fallen in love with Stavros. She also said that he was the only other person apart from me with whom she had ever actually fallen in love. I believed her. From the way she put it I took this as a sort of confession that she had also had other minor affairs with some other men but that in no case was 'love' involved and none had meant much to her. The circumstances of that last trip were such that surely she would not have lied to me. I tried to get all this across to Charles, but I could see that he neither believed whatever Harriet had been saying in those last few days nor that I was not repressing feelings of jealousy which I was denying. The act of sexual union was always important to Harriet all her life, but her capacity for the true selfless feeling of affection and love for another was I believe an emotion she never experienced.

After Charles' third visit I was pleased to overhear him extending an invitation to Sima to go with him to the opera. At the previous lunch the week before we had begun talking about music and about opera in particular. I was telling them of the enormous enthusiasm that my young brother Billy had had for Italian opera. How in particular he loved the vocal enthusiasms of an Italian audience which would erupt so spontaneously at the end or even before the end of any favourite performance. Charles was enthusiastic but I don't think that my daughter was really interested in the subject. There is something about the females in my family and their attitude to music. Starting with Harriet herself and including Anne and Sima and even William's wife, they all pay lip-service to the appreciation of music, but none of them are really involved.

I heard Sima eagerly accepting the invitation and I was aware of them chatting together for over half an hour in the Hall before I heard the front door shut. There are no plans for any further visits and I understand that Charles will be reporting to the CPS shortly.

Chapter 6

Conradin

It is really no use asking me about the last of the Hohenstauffens. History may have become my favourite subject but I never went deeply into the Middle Ages. Apart from knowing that he had the same name as me, the only other fact that I knew about him was that he was murdered at the age of 15 by a wicked Uncle or someone. I too am currently 15 so it is all very dreamy. The murder or the execution or whatever it may have been was carried out with the full blessing and connivance of the then Pope, so my namesake must have been important in some way or another. I don't dislike my name – it does have a sort of aristocratic timbre about it I suppose – so I have accepted it. However it is rather long and within the family it is sometimes shortened to 'Dini', as it helps to differentiate me quickly from my grandfather, whose name is Conrad.

I was living with my father's sister, Anne, during that summer of 1999, just before all the excitement of the millennium. My young cousins were all away, staying with their father in his summer cottage in the south of France for a few weeks. Aunty Anne was living alone, her divorce having just gone through. She was a bit sad and wanted company while her children were away on holiday and invited me to stay with her. I was happy to get away from my mother and father for a week or two. My Dad – William – is a bit of a know-all and not very patient with anyone who has different views to his. I mean we don't quarrel or anything like that, although it is in our family tradition that we argue about everything, but I could never win an argument with him and he was teasing me that summer about some of my ideas.

I had recently got confirmed at school and was, I think, fairly clear about my religious beliefs. I mean I am not that sure about the various aspects of the Trinity and the nature of Christ and all that jazz, but I do find the simpler aspects of Christianity very appealing, and anyway all my school friends – boys and girls – were into the same thing, and we could discuss together all the questions arising from what we were being taught. I really loved chatting about these matters with my friends in my school study room in the afternoons after classes ended.

My mother Angela is a devout Roman Catholic, and her insistence that I went to a Roman Catholic boarding school was one of the very few occasions when she overrode my father. I was never present of course at the discussions which must have taken place when I was about 10 – but I know well what my father's attitude would have been. For him it was all mumbo-jumbo, and whether the host became the literal body of Jesus Christ or it was purely symbolic would have been for him a matter of the utmost indifference – even I could say contempt.

I, however, was full of what I had been recently taught, so that in those summer holidays when I got back from school my Dad irritated me even more than usual by the manner in which he seemed to pour scorn on the more abstruse parts of Christian belief – many of which I was not even aware of. If we were in the company of my grandfather Conrad during one of these discussions, this would be one of the rare occasions on which I would not be supported by him in his inimitable good-hearted manner. I knew of course that Conrad's own grandfather, some grandee or other from Constantinople, had been a notorious unbeliever. But as far as

I was concerned that did not excuse my pompous and opinionated ass of a father, who always thought he knew everything better than anyone else. So I was glad to get away from them for a few weeks to stay with my Aunt, who had begged my Dad to send me round to give her some company if I wasn't doing anything else. In any case I then had more freedom to get around than if I continued staying with my parents.

About two days after I settled down in Anne's house my grandmother Harriet arrived. I don't think that Auntie was expecting her, but that was only a feeling that I had at the time. My grandmother had suffered a major second stroke several months before and had been in Hospital ever since, until quite recently. Her first stroke had impaired her speech and the second stroke had left her in a state of complete dependence on others. She was in her seventies though I am not too sure about her actual age. Grandma had insisted on going home a few weeks previously and Grandpa had arranged for two full-time carers for her. There was now always one of them on duty night and day taking it in turns. Grandpa also helped in looking after her and made a point of being the one taking her out in her wheelchair for a walk. I don't know how or why or in what circumstances she turned up at Auntie's house, as I was not at home when she arrived, but I believed she had asked to go and stay with her daughter, and as this was not far from her own home the two nurses had agreed to be there with her.

As is perhaps clear from my comments about my Dad and our arguments about religion, we are as a family used to talking openly about everything, even things that other families might feel to be inappropriate in front of children. I understand that this may have also stemmed from that same grandee ancestor who believed that everything should be openly discussed in a family – even with children. There was of course a limit, but at 15 there were no such limits left for me. So it was that I was present right from the start to hear the long, often painfully uttered, stuttered I should say, conversations between Harriet and her daughter Auntie Anne. It was clear that they were used to discussing problems with each other and neither of them had the slightest inhibition from saying it all in front of me.

Harriet could not bear her current condition. Her mind was almost as active as before, but many times she could not formulate the words necessary to enable her to communicate. This caused her the most unbearable anguish. She made it clear that she could just about live with the pains involved, though she hated the occasional necessity of having to take strong pain-killers, which then left her mind fuzzy and no longer alert. It was the indignities, as she saw them, of the everyday care that was necessary that drove her 'barmy'. I don't care – that is the exact word I would use. I mean, to be brutally frank, she couldn't wipe her own bottom. I may be only 15, but I really did understand her feelings, and I knew the necessity of immediately disappearing if some bodily function would suddenly arise requiring the presence of my Aunt or one of the nurses. This was not because I had any silly male aversion to being a witness to the more sordid facts of life of that sort, but because I knew with complete certainty that Harriet could not bear to be seen by another man, even an immature grandson, in that predicament.

I have dwelt on all this because I have to follow her, as sympathetically as possible, to her next step. Harriet wanted to die. She craved an end to a life which she was finding unbearable. Her mind was clear and in all the talk with Anne, whenever the nurses were out, and certainly whenever I was present, she was clear, concise and fully aware of what she was saying – always of course subject to the slurred and stuttering speech. As she talked night after night it was clear that the problem was that she was not in any condition to take steps herself to end her unhappy condition. She could do almost nothing for herself. She complained to us both that her body was still in a way strong and that she could not even try to shorten her life by simply refusing medication – as the medication she was taking was only for the purpose of relieving pain, not for the prolongation of life.

Grown-ups have said to me that my grandmother had a self-centred, indeed almost selfish, streak in her. I cannot say that I have myself ever noticed anything like that in her. Whilst she has sometimes seemed a little cool towards my younger sisters, she was always most friendly and pleasant with me. All my grown-up life – well all right since I was fourteen then – I have seen that my Grandpa was always most attentive towards whatever she wanted whenever we were all together, or so it seemed to me.

In the course of one of the discussions during that week Grandma suggested collecting sleeping pills and getting Anne to put them together and give them all at once to her one day. It didn't seem too drastic to me, but in my own immaturity at the time, I did not realise quite how deeply self-centred in a way this very request to Auntie Anne was. Anne herself recoiled in horror and dissolved into tears each time this suggestion was put to her. She herself was in an emotional state as a result of her own recent divorce. I felt desperately sorry for both of them, but of course I never said anything. I did on one occasion reach forward and hold my Aunt's hand tight after Grandma had been wheeled away leav-

ing Anne in quiet tears. Absolutely nothing else was discussed during those days, though Harriet was careful to
keep her thoughts away from the two nurses.

I was in and out of the house, of course, throughout
those two weeks – going up to town and meeting friends
– so I was not present all the time. Harriet's speech remained slurred but she learnt to control it by speaking very slowly and sort of practicing to herself before
she spoke. Anne had arranged for an excellent specially
designed mobile phone to be within her limited reach
and I understand that she had used it several times to
telephone people, not in the family – only on the occasions when she was alone.

After two weeks of all this my Aunt was getting to the
end of her tether – well, cliché or not I don't really know
how else to put it – and was now threatening to ring my
Dad, her brother William, to come and speak to Harriet
herself. It's funny that her thought went towards William to sort it out rather than Conrad who surely was
the one who mattered wasn't he? In fact absolutely not
a word of the situation was ever raised on the days that
Conrad came to visit. Anne's children were shortly due
back from their holiday abroad with their father and it
was clear to all of us including the nurses, though not
to Harriet, that she really would have to return home
before they arrived back.

It was then only two days before I had agreed to go
with Anne to fetch the children from Gatwick – they
were travelling as unaccompanied minors – that Harriet came out with the bombshell that was going to make
such a difference to our lives over the next six months. I
will try to recall exactly those stuttering words as we sat
in the sitting room. The nurse on duty had left and we
were talking about the forthcoming arrival of my cousins – Anne's little boy and girl. Harriet began speaking

and I have written it down as if it was one continuous clear narrative. But, although there was no major interruption from either of us, it was of course punctuated throughout by 'stammers', hesitations, slurred incomprehensible words or near words, repetitions and contradictions, together with stifled comments from Anne. However, in the end this was the gist of what she said –

"My dears, I have been making enquiries – yes, yes, on the telephone of course, what did you think. Enquires all over the world. Don't be silly Anne who cares about telephone bills! It appears that under Swiss law, under certain conditions, Euthanasia is legal. There is a chap called Minelli – I don't know some lawyer or other – who has recently set up a group called 'Dignitas', that will assist its members to die where that member is suffering badly. You have to join of course and become a member and must eventually go to Switzerland to die. Their motto is "To live with dignity: To die with dignity". As far as I have been able to ascertain the group has been in existence for about a year – and also as far as I can tell they will deal with non-Swiss members as well as Swiss."

As I made clear already all this came out in fits and starts, with a lot of hesitations and interruptions. At the end we were all exhausted. Harriet because of the sheer physical effort of getting all those words out in some sort of order, Anne because she was continually in tears and overflowing with emotion, I, well oddly enough I too was exhausted because I was feeling so sorry not so much for Grandma as for Auntie. Grandma herself was in a state of a sort of euphoric triumph and was clearly irritated by her daughter's tears. Her last words just before she was wheeled away, words which were delivered very firmly and for the first time without any slurring or stammering, I recall in clear detail –

"I am going home tomorrow, Anne. One thing I know, I may not be able to rely on you lot, but I know I can always rely on my Conrad."

Chapter 7

William

I still can't believe how long it took before my obstinate son decided to tell me what had been going on whilst he was staying with my sister Anne. I had no problem at all with the fact that my mother chose to unburden herself first to her daughter rather than speaking to me or for that matter to my Dad. But for Conradin to have remained silent all that time and not seen how his Aunt was suffering is not acceptable. He could have phoned me at any time. I certainly made sure he knew of my anger at his immaturity the day he finally did return home and poured out all the details of what had been happening. We had the usual hard words which ended when he flounced upstairs in a sulk, went into his room and turned his music on far too loud.

My first reaction when I heard what Mama was contemplating was to google 'Dignitas' and try to find out what all this was about. This was still 1999 and I discovered that the Organisation, registered in Switzerland, had only been in existence for about a year and was run by a Swiss lawyer called Minelli. This is the gist of what I found on their own website, and really I can do no better than to quote it verbatim.

Anyone suffering from an illness which will lead inevitably to death, or anyone with an unendurable disability, who wants voluntarily to put an end to their life and suffering can, as a member of DIGNITAS, request the association to help them with accompanied suicide.

DIGNITAS procures the necessary medication for this, a lethal, fast-acting and completely painless barbiturate which is dissolved in ordinary drinking water. After taking it, the patient falls asleep within a few minutes, after which sleep passes peacefully and completely painlessly into death.

Naturally, each permitted use of this fatally effective medication requires a Swiss doctor's prescription, for only by this means can the drug legally be procured....... for people who are not resident in Switzerland, DIGNITAS calls on doctors who cooperate with DIGNITAS. After an in-depth evaluation of the member's written request and medical information, and following at least two face-to-face meetings with the member (which allows the DIGNITAS doctor to satisfy him- or herself that the member meets the pre-conditions for the desired accompanied suicide) the prescription may be issued to DIGNITAS.

From this time onwards, the member wishing to die can arrange the time of their accompanied suicide with DIGNITAS. There are always at least two people present at an accompanied suicide: they can then testify as to the course of events.

Frequently, members want to die in the company of those closest to them. DIGNITAS emphasizes the importance of involving friends and relatives in the process: the "long journey" that is assisted dying requires careful preparation for and consideration of the appropriate time to say farewell.

All right, all right I can't help it. I am a lawyer and years of conditioning means that before I comment on anything I have to get the facts right. Furthermore, in view of my own attitude towards these people I feel that in fairness I have to set out their position accurately first.

The website goes on in a very reasonable manner, setting out how the Association deals with non-Swiss residents as opposed to Swiss residents. It lists all sorts of caveats relating to the medical evidence required, and it makes it clear how carefully any requests will be screened. I had to accept that I could find no evidence of what I would call 'quackery', or any evidence of any fraudulent nature. Finally, armed with all the information I could find, I went to visit my parents, first warning my sister Sima when I was coming.

However, when I arrived it immediately became clear that Harriet had not said a word to Conrad. Conrad had made all sorts of changes to the house, which enabled my mother to live on the ground floor so that she could be easily wheeled into the sitting room at any time. That way she could take part as best as she could in family discussions and meet such visitors as she might want to see – all without the paraphernalia of getting people to go upstairs to a bedroom. It seemed to me that my Dad was coping well and that accordingly, now that Mum was being looked after by a loving husband, she was getting reconciled to a condition which was going to last for the rest of her life.

But Conrad was doing the looking-after mentally – not physically. I know that Conrad would have been quite prepared to deal with the physical aspects without any qualms or reservations whatsoever, but it was Harriet herself who could not bear to have that sort of help from anyone in her family, particularly any of the men. I am not sure that I understood why. I really couldn't explain it, but it was clear that she wanted professional help. I suppose she could not trust the sort of nursing care the family could provide. In one of our discussions about all this, my son said I was talking nonsense and that he understood totally where Grandma was coming from as he put it. Impudent lad – what did he know at his age.

So, when I saw how things were on that first trip I thought that either Conradin had been exaggerating, or that once Harriet got home, she had changed her mind. Needless to say I kept quiet of course and was thankful that matters had not gone further, and that I had no reason to intervene in any way. I thought it was all over, but I was wrong. About a week later I got a call from a very distressed Sima asking me to drop everything and come to the house right away.

When I arrived Mother was in the sitting-room, sitting in her wheelchair as upright as she could get. Conrad was standing behind her with one hand on her shoulder, which of course she herself could not have felt. Sima was sitting opposite them, flushed but without any tears so far as I could see. Even as a child I can never remember Sima crying. In the midst of Anne's elder sibling teasing, people shouting at her, bullying by me, Nikko's tantrums, she would remain as solid as a rock. But her anger would simmer. Whilst the rest of us would quickly forget our tantrums or sulks she would remain stubbornly angry at whatever it was that was causing the rest of us to burst out with our emotions. It might take days for her to get over it.

I had let myself in and walked straight into what appeared to be a strained silence. Harriet looked round – or rather just managed to swivel her neck enough to see me at the door and said –

"Ah William " – then after a short silence – "Come, son, don't pretend to look surprised, you can't fool me you know. You know perfectly well what all this is about because Conradin would have told you."

"Mother – it's all right – it's all right – speak more slowly, take your time. No need to swallow to get the next word out. Now what's going on. Are you still obsessed with this ridiculous Switzerland thing."

"I am not obsessed with anything – I am not thinking of doing something, I am certain. I cannot bear this wheelchair any longer; I can't bear the mental anguish; I can't live with the daily, hourly indignities. I am over 70, I've had my life and I can be thankful that it has been a good one."

I should make it clear that as we stood listening to her we were not hearing the words as I have written them down. The words were coming out in stops and starts, with hesitations and gasping effort, with stutters and silences as Mum tried to form the next words – but I can only set down the final meaning – and the clarity and the meanings were throughout as clear as a bell.

"I've had my life, William, its not as if I was young and can still think of doing something, of being someone. All I have left is a long and painful drag until I die naturally. Why? Just tell me why I shouldn't just end it all peacefully and at a time I choose."

"Because, Mama, you are surrounded by people who love you and......"

"Fiddlesticks – banal hypocrisy! You've all had plenty of my love all your lives – all of you. And yes, yes, I've had plenty of love from you all in return. But it's over, I say, it's over. I want out."

Sima was as close to tears as I have ever seen her but was not saying a word. Conrad stood still as a statue, holding on to Harriet's shoulder, but also not saying a word.

I didn't need to hear what he thought. I knew my father well. Tolerant and not quick to anger, he had a military sense of duty that he got from his father. This sense of duty would have been reinforced during his wartime service with the army between 1941 and 1948. Suicide for him would be a sort of dereliction of duty – deserting the battlefield – letting down the troops, akin almost to desertion in the face of the enemy. But this attitude is one that he would apply to himself, and perhaps to his peers. The situation here was however his own wife and completely different criteria would be sure to apply.

At the painful end of Harriet's latest declaration about love there was another silence. Then Harriet, now speaking more slowly and managing her words a bit better, though always with the fits and starts of her condition said –

"Look – I know I was wrong to ask Anne to collect up and give me some sleeping pills – I wasn't thinking – I wasn't thinking. But I am helpless, I can do nothing for myself. I am suffering and I am scared stiff that another stroke will then leave me with my brain still intact, but unable then even to move or feel anything or to communicate with anyone. Don't for God's sake talk to me about 'love' – or the comforts of 'love'. Without any senses left, sight gone, hearing gone, speech gone, totally helpless, who cares a monkey's fart about the love of the people staring down at you."

At this point Conrad squeezed Harriet's shoulder and came round to her front. He sat down on the sofa and motioned me to come and sit also. He smiled at her, and she made an effort to smile back – a rictus formed in her semi-paralysed lips which made do as a smile. Quietly and without any great emphasis he said, and it was clear that his words had been thought out throughout the previous fifteen minutes –

"My darling before I say another word, please understand that I am ready, as I always have been, to do whatever will make you happy. I am ready to help you. No, don't say a word, just believe that. But you must see that I must first be absolutely certain that this is truly what you want and that nothing will change your mind. I know, I know, don't mutter at me, I know you mean it! But a few more months isn't going to make all that much of a difference. The sheer administrative process is going to take weeks or months anyway. Look at me – look at me Harriet. Do you accept that in the end, once satisfied, I will do as you ask. Just nod your head."

Well, I saw her do so, and it was then that I knew that I had to intervene.

I know I may not be as 'touchy-feely' and sensitive as my sisters or my ebullient younger brother Nikko. I know that I am a bit pedantic. I have after all had twenty years of legal training and I can't get all that out of my head or out of my character.. At this stage in the family discussions I had only just become involved, although I had come to it forewarned as a result of what Conradin had told me. I realised that in the midst of all the emotion flowing around us, I had to deal with one particular aspect of the situation that had so far not been taken into account by anyone. I had to make clear to my parents what the Law in England and Wales said about assisted suicide. So, after Conrad had finished speaking I got up. I felt, I don't know why, that I could not remain seated in what I was about to say –

"Listen, mother, I want to say something. You won't like it, but I must be crystal clear that both you and Dad understand what I am saying. In this country it is a direct criminal offence to encourage or assist a suicide, or assist in any attempted suicide. There are no ifs or buts in what I have just said. The Suicide Act, passed about forty years ago, is still in full force. I can reproduce the words exactly because I have looked it up and read and re-read it over and over during the last week. It provides that it is a 'criminal offence to aid, abet, counsel or procure the suicide of another person'. It refers to a maximum of fourteen years imprisonment."

"Oh come on William," said Conrad, "are they really going to chase up people who might help Mummy to go to Geneva or wherever."

"Yes, Dad, Yes! So far as I have been able to ascertain no one from this country has as yet taken this way out, by going to Switzerland. This Dignitas thing has only been in existence for a year or so. But I have no doubt at all that once somebody does apply to join Dignitas and does go, the Law will need clarification and anyone assisting that person will be prosecuted and imprisoned if found guilty."

After this the discussion on that first occasion got a bit heated and went all over the place. My point made no impression on either of my parents and even less on Sima. Over the next six months as the debate within the family shifted and widened my own narrowly legalistic approach got short shrift, and from my son Conradin outright hostility and youthful contempt. But I have to insist that it was not just narrow legalism. The law exists primarily to protect its citizens and whether you like it or not this was the law of the land we lived in. It could not simply be ignored as if the Law was to have no effect at all on how we should or should not behave. Everyone is entitled to make every effort to lobby parliament to change such laws as he thinks are wrong, that is what defines democracy. But the citizen of a country living under the rule of law cannot pick and chose those actual laws which he decides to obey and reject those he doesn't like.

There was another aspect which had an influence on me. I knew my father better than I think any of the rest of the family, including Mum. In the extraordinary moral maze which revolved round Harriet's wish to commit suicide and to apply euthanasia, my Dad would get comfort by following what the law dictated. Despite having come back from the Yugoslav conflict bitter and disillusioned about the NATO intervention, my Dad was not a natural rebel. He had a wish to conform so long as it did not offend his principles. I thought that by emphasising what the Law said about assisted suicide that would make it easier for him to fall back on what would have been his likely attitude to suicide in the first place.

In case of any doubt I was not only sure of what the Law of England was on this issue – but I also agreed with that Law. Allowing people without any preventative controls to help others to die, voluntary or not, was the start of a dreadful slippery slope which could easily give rise to the most dreadful consequences if allowed to exist unchecked.

I remained clear on this attitude throughout that Autumn, and I thought that I was influencing Conrad and that he too would fall back on the Law, but I was totally wrong. One day, just before Xmas that year, I was again tackling him on the subject., when he stopped, and took my arm and I knew I was about to get a final definitive reply to all my arguments –

"William, my son, I understand what the law of my country says but if I cannot in the end get my wife to change her mind I will follow my conscience and disobey the law. As some recent philosopher said – 'If I ever have to face the choice of betraying my country, or betraying my neighbour, I hope that I would have the moral courage to betray my country'."

Whether that comment is relevant to our situation or not I must say clearly, as my Dad knows well, that I could not agree with him then; nor can I agree with him now. How could he possibly square that comment with his honourable career as a soldier in the British Army. British officers are not supposed to come out with such opinions. I'm sure that I don't need to add that my own son Conradin totally disagrees with me.

Chapter 8

Rasimir

I once heard a grown-up make the comment that the most valuable capital that you can leave to your children is a happy childhood. I have to accept that I was given that, though I don't think that it has helped me in the long run. My parents undoubtedly did their best for me until events became too much for them.

My father, Anton, was a professor of history at Zagreb University. Well I think perhaps that he was not actually a professor – I mean he was not in charge of the History Department or anything like that – he was a Reader or a Senior Lecturer or something like that, but our neighbours always referred to him as 'the professor' and so that was how I thought of him. My dad's work was regular and was fairly well paid, so that my Mum didn't have to work. Mum was not very well educated – she could of course read and write well, as did all her generation. Basic universal education was the one unquestionable success of communist Yugoslavia. But Mum came from a Serbian peasant background and had not had any higher learning. Her parents had a small farm in the rugged Bosnian countryside near Visegrad. Mother had an exaggerated respect for my Dad's erudition and his position at the University and would never contradict him, at least never in front of me.

Mum was never fond of city life and we went out to my Dad's parents in the Croatian countryside regularly at weekends. They had a lovely large house in a completely rural area about an hour's drive away from Zagreb. But they were not farmers or anything like that. I'm not sure what if anything my grandfather did, but I suppose it was something literary as they had an enormous library with sumptuous large easy chairs, and with walls covered right up to the ceiling with books. I spent many a rainy afternoon buried in one of those leather armchairs looking at books which I would have randomly selected. My grandfather said that I could pick out and look at any book so long as I put it back exactly where I found it. He gave me a sort of bright yellow wooden block, and I would push that into the space when I took a book, so it was easy to find when the time came to put the book back.

My Dad, who was the youngest child, had a brother and two sisters, each of whom were married and also had children. They too often came to stay with Grandpa and Grandma, so I usually had lots of cousins to play with when we came. They were all older than me. The girls were always very kind to me as I was so obviously the youngest and there was never any question of the bigger boys bullying me in any way. If they did sometimes make a disparaging remark, the sisters would stop them at once.

This was a very grand house with a middle bit and two wings. One of the wings contained a little chapel which had its own entrance facing towards the main gates of the house, but which also had a little door which led into the house.. Once a month Grandpa arranged for a local priest to come in on a Sunday morning and take Mass. Of course if we were there that particular weekend I would attend with my mother. Mother was a Serb and belonged to the Serbian Orthodox Church, but she was a true believer and would attend this Roman Catholic service. She would push me forward to receive a blessing when the Priest gave communion to the rest of the family but she herself didn't go forward.

My Dad? Well he was a Croat and had of course been

born into the Roman Catholic church and had been baptized and confirmed – but he refused to attend and actually got irritated that mother would go out of respect to Grandpa and Grandma. I don't think that he was a committed Communist, but he was certainly a committed Atheist, much to Grandpa' s displeasure. However, all the cousins cheerfully trooped into the little chapel, together with the servants and together also with some of the villagers who lived nearby.

My father was extremely protective towards mother whenever we were in Grandpa's great house. This was not because she was the only Serb in a household of Croats – Grandpa was far too aristocratic to indulge in that sort of petty bourgeois nationalism and everyone was fully aware that despite his having originally opposed the marriage he would now be extremely angry if anyone disparaged his daughter-in-law in that way in his house. No, my father kept a wary eye out for Mum because she was clearly not as sophisticated or well-educated as all his siblings and their spouses. For her part, she had a deep respect for him and never contradicted him in company. I think that both Grandpa and Grandma liked this in her. I loved the weekends that we spent with them there.

In Zagreb I went to the local school and I had some really good friends in my class. We were about 30 in both the two classes which I attended. We were a mixed school with mixed classes. Whilst most of us were Croats, there were also four Muslim boys and three Serbs. I was very happy there until the great changes of 1992. There was no bullying – no ganging-up, and I recall that our teachers were kind. I made a lot of good friends and we visited each other, though my mother was always a bit nervous if I was ever away at teatime. If I was with a friend who lived on the same road I would be allowed to come home, by 6.00pm of course, on my own. But if I was further away and would have to cross streets, my Mum would require Anton, my Dad, to pick me up on his way home from work.

The weather always seemed to be gloriously sunny.

In the school holidays we would go to visit my Serbian grandparents. They had a small farm in the Bosnian mountains near Visegrad. In those days there was a small local narrow-gauge railway line that ran from Sarajevo to Visegrad. We would take the train from Zagreb to Sarajevo. This would take almost the whole day and we would stop the night with friends of Mum in that town. I only recall that they were a Muslim family. Then the next day, we would take the little local train to Visegrad.

My Serbian grandparents lived in and worked a small farm set in the mountainous country in the South-Eastern corner of Bosnia close to the old frontier with Serbia. It could not have been a greater contrast with the grand country house of my Croatian grandparents. The farm was a ramshackle one-storey stone building, to which other stone sheds were haphazardly attached housing animals of differing shapes and sizes, but mostly pigs of contrasting breeds. The farmyard was always muddy and I happily squelched about in it most of the day. My Dad did not like it much and I think he only came with us once. Here the local boys in the other farms or in the village further down the valley, were either Serbs or Bosnian Muslims. Whereas in Zagreb my Mum was always worried as to where I was and who I was with, here I was free to wander about all day and she was never worried.

It was odd – I was always being told by my Grandpa horrific stories of what their Muslim neighbours who had supported the Croat Ustashe government during the war had done to his Serb friends and neighbours. At the same time I heard from the Muslim boys how they were always being told horror stories about what the Chetniks did to their fathers during the same period. Yet when the boys came clattering out of the village school, which they all attended together, I would be waiting at the gates – the Zagreb schools had closed earlier – we went off on our adventures without a single thought as to who was what, or whose fathers did what to whom. For some time when I first started going there, I was a bit of a curiosity – the only Croat, or rather half Croat boy in the area – but my Grandparents were well known, even if they were dirt-poor like everyone else, and this oddity factor soon disappeared.

I loved it all – one beautiful day after another, with so many friends of all the different communities with whom to have adventures. One day a new Mosque had been opened and I recall running in and out of a festival organised by the Muslim community. The music provided was with flutes and drums. Boys and girls, some dressed in folk costume, danced the local dance – forward and back – sidestep and again forward and back and sidestep all holding hands in a huge line led by a man holding aloft a white handkerchief. We younger boys ran bare-footed around the snaking line, while the older non-muslim boys stood watching and showing off for the girls. The Muslim men were not supposed to be drinking on what was supposedly a religious festival – but some of them slipped off occasionally to join some Serb friend standing watching at the edges of the party to take from him some sneaky shots of the local plum brandy and then slip back to rejoin the dancing.

I am not forgetting the fact that brawls certainly took place – but even at the age of ten I had heard of Tito's law that stated that if anyone dared to utter an unkind bad word to his neighbour based on his ethnic nationality, he would go to prison for ten days – and this was doubled if the unkind word referred to that person's mother. Brawls there were - but look we have seen the internet and they were really not much worse than drink-induced brawls everywhere.

I was given a good capital.

But then came Tudjman and Milosevic and that accumulated capital of a happy childhood evaporated. I am still not sure quite why it disappeared so quickly,

Chapter 9

Conrad

As one way or another Yugoslavia in general and Sarajevo in particular has loomed so large in my family story, my reminiscences as I sat waiting for the CPS to make up its collective mind following on the assisted death of Harriet, turned to that unhappy country and my many experiences there.

I was already in my sixties when the break-up of Yugoslavia, anticipated by so many after the death of Tito, began in the Nineteen-nineties. I was still working for the Newspaper and I agreed to go and cover the situation. This was near the beginning of the crisis and I decided to make my base in Zagreb, rather than trying to cover the developments from Belgrade. Zagreb was easier to get to and frankly was a more attractive city than the rather grim Belgrade.

From the very start I found myself being forced to keep bearing in mind the well-known observation by George Orwell, written in an essay printed in 1948, in which he was commenting on the state of mind of the fanatic nationalist. Based as I was in Zagreb, I watched Tudjman in speech after speech trying to persuade his fellow Croats to get more and more excited and outraged about their relationship with their Serb neighbours with whom they shared a common language. Orwell had observed in that essay -

"The nationalist not only does not disapprove of atrocities committed by his own side, but he or she has quite the most remarkable capacity for never even having heard about them."

It was a comment that applied in 1948 to both sides

in the Palestine conflict, and it applied equally to all parties in the Yugoslav imbroglio.

It was an extraordinarily difficult struggle to cover. It was a conflict during which, when reporting in my articles, I had to overcome my own unconscious prejudices right from the start. I had been stationed in Trieste as an Intelligence Officer in the British Army for over a year after the end of the War. I had witnessed at first hand the ghastly aftermath of the dying moments of the Ustashe government of the large independent state of Croatia created by Nazi Germany following the defeat and conquest of what we might refer to as the first Yugoslavia.

Like so many others who heard it at the time, as a green new officer stationed in Cairo in 1941, I had been thrilled by the news of the revolt in Belgrade when the Serbs had refused to accept the German Diktat requiring them to allow the passage of German armed forces through Yugoslavia to march into Greece in order to come to the rescue of the faltering Italian invasion. I had been moved by Churchill's stirring words when he announced on the radio –

"Early this morning the Yugoslav nation found its soul. A revolution has broken out in Belgrade and the feeble ministers who but yesterday" -(isn't that phrase just pure Churchill)- "signed away the freedom and honour of their country, are now themselves under arrest."

Both I, and all my young fellow-officers stationed in Cairo at that time were highly excited by the coup d'etat in Belgrade. We were already cock-a-hoop about the Greeks standing up to Mussolini's bullying and then driving back his demoralised army into the Albanian mountains. We felt that it was very rare in history that events could occur as a result of the entirely spontaneous and enthusiastic actions of ordinary people. This two-fingers gesture to Hitler by the people of Belgrade was surely one of those rare moments. Germany was undoubtedly at that moment the mightiest military power in the whole world and would now certainly fall upon Yugoslavia and crush it with all its power – and no one could help them. But what a magnificent gesture – and how hopelessly, gloriously, typically Serb!

It is remarkable how deeply these impressions, formed when we were young, get into our unconscious. Our cultural and historical memories run deep and this of course apples as much to a Croat or a Serb as to myself. We have fought two world wars against the Germans and in both of them Croatia had a natural affinity with Germany, whilst Serbia was or became an ally of Britain and France. It really is therefore no accident that as Yugoslavia began to break up modern democratic Germany supported the break-up, whilst the British and French were not so sure.

The old frontier between the Ottoman Empire and the Hapsburgs of Austria-Hungary in the Balkans was, and in some way remains, one of the great fault-lines of division in Europe. North of the line the alphabet is Latin, south it is Cyrillic; north of the line the religion is Roman Catholic, south it is Orthodox; north of the line the history is that of being part of the feudal German-dominated Austrian Empire, south of the line the experience is of centuries of Ottoman domination with an entirely different type of social structure. Then right there, in some cases even straddling the line both north and south of it, with a common language and a common racial background but with little else in common, stand the Serbs and the Croats.

Look, I was only eighteen when I listened to that speech by Churchill – after which we all got drunk. I do now realise that perhaps that dry old Croat professor was right when he pointed out that Churchill was wrong to talk about "the soul of the Yugoslav nation" as no such 'nation' existed, so far as he could see. But for us at the time, all we could see was two little countries – Greece and Yugoslavia - standing up to the military might of Germany, and the jackal mentality of its ally Italy.

During that first break-up of Yugoslavia in the 1940's what had been a single country was divided up by the German conquerors into seven or more different units. What constituted the Slovene section, for example, always the most easily differentiated of the constituent parts of the country, was partitioned between Germany and Italy. An independent state of Croatia came into existence to be led by a Croat nationalist – one Ante Pavelic – an out and out anti-Semitic Fascist, who had long been exiled in Italy but who had established a following amongst some Croats dissatisfied with the admittedly Serb-dominated government of Royal Yugoslavia.

Once the Germans took over the country, the establishment of new authorities throughout the country was accompanied by a whole spate of settling of old accounts. The Ustashe turned their own territory, which not only included the historic area of old Croatia, but also most of Bosnia-Herzegovina, into a slaughterhouse. They unleashed a terror against the Serbian villages of the Krajina, and the mixed Serbian-Moslem villages of Bosnia as well, forcing the peasants into the choice of either being massacred in their old ancestral homes by the Ustashe militia and police, or of joining the partisans and fighting. So it was that many joined the Communist partisans. In view of the tone of my preceding paragraphs, it is worth bearing in mind that Tito was himself half-Croat, that he was supported by many

Croats, and that the Croats who supported Pavelic were always a minority.

Nevertheless I have to make it clear that the terror in Croatia was directed not only against all the usual targets of a fascist-nationalistic party – Jews, homosexuals, political opponents and the rest - but also specifically against Serbs. Pavelic wanted a final solution of what he saw as the great problem. His agenda required the forced conversion of a third of them by getting them to become Roman Catholic, the forced expulsion of another third, and the killing of all the rest. As an example of the Pavelic regime I am just going to quote the first clause of the Law for the Defence of the People decreed in Zagreb. This stated –

"Whosoever in whatever manner offends or has offended against the honour and interests of the Croat nation….whether in deed or in mere intent, this person has committed the crime of high treason."

This Law allowed for retroactive prosecution, and as it did not define 'honour and interests of the Croat nation' it basically allowed the Ustashe to proceed against anyone. And they did; setting up kangaroo courts to deal with all the hundreds who had overnight become 'traitors'.

I have been reflecting on this period of my life largely because of the attitude my son William has taken in respect of my wife's wish to end her own life. I always knew in my heart from the beginning of all the family discussions, that in the end I would rather disregard the strict laws of my country rather than let down my wife. What has all that got to do with Yugoslavia one might say? Well, I am after all in the process of reflecting on my past, ever since being arrested. The last few years of my life have brought me to the position that I am facing today, and what happened in Yugoslavia and what I saw there has clearly affected my stance, and so is relevant.

It was the NATO bombing offensive against the civilian population of Serbia which was the final twist of the situation in the former Yugoslavia, and which, conflicting with years of military training and discipline, converted me once and for all against this sort of arrogant military intervention. I do accept, that the manner in which that walking catastrophe - Milosevic – had been acting against the Albanians in Kosovo, was fairly outrageous. After all I personally witnessed it and reported on it myself. But it was all very well for Blair and Clinton and the rest of the smug Western world to talk about how the world had changed and how matters of humanitarian concern now overrode national sovereignty – but would they have acted in the same way in the event say of atrocities being carried out by the Turkish government against a Kurdish minority, or an Indian government oppressing some Assamese tribes.

The NATO bombing campaign was a disgraceful act of terror in which smug self-satisfied Westerners – sure of their own high moral position – sent their young men to bomb people in order to satisfy their own consciences. There were no grounds of high national policy, which might after all be defended for reasons of national realpolitick. All that bombing was done simply to satisfy the tender scruples of their electorates, as they read their morning papers and felt 'outraged'. It was in a sense made worse by the fact that in no way was the action allowed to have the possible effect of having bodybags brought back, which might have had a negative effect on their constituents.

I come from a military family. My father was a Naval officer all his working life. My grandfather was in the army and retired as a Colonel. I myself served in the Army for seven years of warfare, a war which I considered and still consider to have been necessary and justified. But the idea that military officers never think for themselves is a complete nonsense spread about and believed only by the left. It is one militarily vital thing to maintain iron-hard, unthinking discipline in situations of team conflict; it is quite another to be able to take a hard moral look at what your civilian government is requiring you to do.

Even before what I witnessed in the former Yugoslavia I have never entirely understood the attitude shown by the Anglo-Saxon public to the terror bombing of civilians. I will pose two situations. On the one hand the men who send a young man, without any anger or passion, to simply do his job, to press a button from a mile away up in the sky, and to release a bomb which may or may not then fall upon a house, a school, or a factory or some strategic bridge, inevitably almost always killing and maiming possibly many people. On the other hand the men who in a passion of violent rage offer an amnesty to a group of elderly peasants if they agree to convert to Roman Catholicism, then cutting their throats and clubbing them to death when they turn up for the conversion ceremony – an event which actually happened. I have of course deliberately chosen a particularly nasty example in order, as it were, to make the airman's action as ordered by his superiors look even better by comparison.

I am quite certain that faced with these two situations the vast majority of Westerners would mumble about ' the inevitable exigencies and requirements of legitimate warfare' in respect of the strategic decision to send the clean-cut young man up to press his button, whilst totally condemning the unshaven Croat or Serb, say, cutting the throat of a Bosnian Muslim. In both cases, both the clean-cut young pilot in his state of the art aeroplane a mile high in the air, and the desperate, hungry, unshaven, Serb or Croat on the ground have of course been manipulated by wiser and older men. But it is a complete hypocrisy to claim that the men manipulating the airmen are in a vastly stronger moral position than the men manipulating the guerrillas or whatever on the ground.

The bombing of Dresden, three months before the end of the war is, I suppose, the ultimate and most blatant example of the culmination of a bombing campaign designed very specifically as a weapon of terror directed against the civilian population of an enemy, with the ultimate object of trying to achieve victory by some sort of regime change brought about by fear. At Dresden there was no strategic objective other than pure terror, there were no factories or vital transport links, the town was crowded with desperate refugees fleeing from the advancing Red Army, Germany was facing absolute and total defeat within days and the bombing did not speed up that defeat by even a minute. My view is that that was as bad a war crime as any Croat General or Serb megalomaniac had to face at the Hague.

The Great Powers have continually meddled, entirely in their own interests, in the Balkans, particularly in those areas originally controlled by the decaying, sometimes cruel but basically multi-national Ottoman Empire. In doing so they have created and fostered a myth, very widespread in Western Europe, that the indigent peoples of the area are primitives and have hated each other and fought against each other for centuries. It is simply not so – though superficially it might appear so.

I recall my father complaining about how it was suggested that in Crete, for instance, the Muslim population and the Christian population could not live together – and that in parts of Anatolia the old-established

Greek population and the Turks could not live together either. Ergo it was an act of statesmanship to force them to be separated. My Dad always recalled that this forced exchange of populations was settled by the Treaty of Lausanne which it seems was signed on the actual day that I was born. But these people had lived together for centuries under the Ottomans. They may not have been buddy-buddies, but they got along and their lives were enriched by the variety of people among whom they lived.

It was exactly the same in the Balkans – in the former Yugoslavia.

Whilst I was there in the early nineties, the accepted figure for Bosnia produced from the last country-wide census before the break-up, was that thirty-two per cent of marriages in the urban areas in the province were 'mixed marriages'. Thirty per cent! Despite what Western journalists and politicians declaimed – this is not the stuff of 'ancestral tribal hatreds'. I witnessed it myself. Time and again I came across couples forced into having to make heart-breaking choices by Milosevic's devious nationalist manoeuvrings, motivated only by his requirement to retain power for himself, on the one hand, and Tudjman's blundering nationalist ranting on the other.

I said it several times in the articles which I sent home during that time. You may hate your neighbour for all sorts of rational or irrational reasons, but to hate a whole community requires manipulation – governmental, nationalist, or religious manipulation. It is easy to condemn Pavelic. There were plenty of honourable Croats, Tito amongst them, who opposed him at the time, some losing their lives in the process. But, apart from the vicious brutality, was Tudjman philosophically much better – the rationale behind his ranting was much the same. Nor, I hasten to add, was Milosevic any better!

I sit at my desk these days waiting for the CPS to make up it's mind as to what to do about my crime and I reflect about the break-up of what we might call the second Yugoslavia – Tito's Yugoslavia. My opinion is that Tito fashioned a state in which a serious attempt was made to reconcile differences between people. Whilst I have denied the 'uncivilised ancestral tribal hatreds' so beloved of the West, I do not belittle the differences that did exist. Tito tried to mould a state taking into account those differences, which could after all also be an element of energy and stimulation. It was a real attempt to contain the worst excesses of the one-people, one volk, one religion, nation-state. It failed, largely because it went together with the breakdown of Marxist theory, but there was nothing inevitable about the failure.

I recall one day taking a cycle trip into the countryside in the north-western corner of Bosnia. It was in the early nineties and during the final ethnic cleansing of the Serbs from that particular area. I stayed the night with a delightful Croat family in Petrinja – a half-Serb half-Croat little town – large village really. The family I lodged with for a couple of days before I cycled on, consisted only of a mother, a grandmother and two little boys aged nine and ten. The father and the grandfather of the family had been killed in some fairly gruesome way – shot or stabbed – this time by Serbs. I went for a walk the second morning with the two boys both of whom knew a little English and as we walked they pointed out to me houses which had been shelled by 'our guns' as they put it, and were now in ruins. They told me stories as they tripped gaily along, stories about decapitations, heads being stuck on poles, limbs hacked off, eyes gouged out – all virtually identical to horror stories going round in almost every corner of the whole country. I'm not saying that there was no truth at all in some of these stories –but they were certainly not true of this particular village, as a friendly educated adult did confirm to me.

Once leaders start trying to bring out the worst in their followers, they can be very successful. This little story shows how easy it is to manipulate people. What upset me the most about this experience, and which I am recalling vividly 7 or 8 years later, is that these false details of throat-slashings and shootings were being re-counted to me by two delightful little boys – a genera-tion deliberately being brought up to fear a people who were once their fellow-citizens in a united country. As we walked, the boys cavorted themselves around me, they giggled and threw stones into the river and were boyish and charming, at the same time as they were dispassionately recounting what they thought they had actually seen.

A few days later when I was back in Sarajevo, I met an elderly woman in the market who had sad haunted eyes. She said to me –

"Before the advent of Tudjman and Milosevic, before the great Western Powers started meddling and selling us all their arms, we here in Sarajevo were creatively mixed. Now we are destructively mixed."

I say now – as I said then – that Lord Acton was right when he wrote –

"The principle of universal national self-determina-tion in the form of the nation-state was and remains a retrograde step in history."

Chapter 10

Conrad

Here I am waiting to see if I am going to be prosecuted by the CPS for a matter on which I feel no guilt of any kind. It is no use William going on about my identity as an English citizen and the necessity to conform to the laws of the country in which I was born. I certainly don't define my identity as depending on the laws of any particular nation-state. Ah, identity? The majority of people, born in the village or town where their parents were also born, have no problem with identity. This applies as equally to the caste Hindu Indian villager born somewhere in Bihar, as to the middle class Englishman born somewhere in the Home Counties. The problem arises when the caste Indian is born in the Home Counties, or when the Englishman is born in Bihar. There is a pull both ways, and it is facile to go on about which cricket team you support. There is a split in your identity whether you like it or not, which will probably not concern the next generation.

The one aspect upon which I believe most people would agree is that it has nothing to do with blood lines. But soft, is that also entirely true. Consider a little English boy, English genes both sides, born to English missionaries in the middle of China during the great troubles of the civil wars. His parents die, leaving him abandoned in all that chaos as the Japanese invade, and he is brought up from the age of two or whatever by a loving Chinese couple, who treat him exactly like one of their own children. Will his identity be wholly Chinese, or will some of his genes come out in character? For myself, I start from the clear premise that I was born in London in 1923 on the very day that the Turks and Greeks signed the Treaty of Lausanne, beginning the process of 'exchange of populations' which became such a totally negative feature of the twentieth century. My mother, born Olga Avakian a subject of the Ottoman Empire, was Armenian – completely, on both sides, and going back a long way. My father was an English naval officer. What did that make me? During most of my life I had not thought much about it. Wherever you are and whatever your problems, you tend to get on with your life without too much analysis. But as I approach the twilight of my life, I think about it more, and above all, I had to face it rather violently about six years ago.

I can't now remember the exact date of the events that I am recalling, but it was sometime in the early nineties when I returned from my first stint of reporting from the disintegrating Yugoslavia. My editor called me in and asked if I could go out again on a new assignment. The conversation went something like this –

"Conrad – you've got connections with Istanbul haven't you. Weren't you born there or something?

"No, John, I was born right here near Regents Park if you want to know. Why, what's up?

"The fact is that Turkey is in the news and we need someone to go out there and send back a few articles. There are two matters on which we need to concentrate. First I would like a few in-depth articles about the average Turk's attitude to their application to join the EU. You know - with your usual touch of personal human interest stories. But secondly – and this is where your recent experience will come in - I need stuff about the current Turkish attitudes to the crisis in Bosnia."

"Why?"

"Well – you know of course of the current switch in the Bosnian crisis. The Croat-Muslim agreement has collapsed, and the Croats are now bombarding the Bosniak side of Mostar. This has aroused a lot of interest in the Muslim world. The Croats have demolished the well-known Ottoman bridge that connects the two sides of the city – and this bridge is a famous icon of the Ottoman years. It would be interesting to see what reaction there is, if any from modern Turkey."

"Frankly John," I had replied, "I don't think that they are that interested. In an odd sort of way they have turned their backs on the Ottoman period. Everything for them starts with Kemal and 1923."

"Never mind – just go and see for yourself. The fact that your mother was Armenian isn't going to be a problem for you is it?"

"No it won't I'm sure. But look John, Harriet has always wanted to visit Istanbul to see where my mother's family came from – can the expenses run to her coming with me. A hotel room for two isn't much more than for one."

Well, my editor grumbled but I knew he would end up agreeing. So it was that for the first time for over fifty years I arrived in an Istanbul that I scarcely recognised. My last trip was with my parents in the summer of 1939 when we only just managed to get away in time on one of the last trains to leave the city before the war broke out. I was returning in quite different circumstances and to a very different city.

My expertise throughout my journalistic career had been the Middle East and the Balkans. But in addition, my experience as a British officer during the Palestine mandate, my knowledge of Arabic as well as several other languages, and my general background with family in Istanbul had all proved very useful and I had become known by a fairly sophisticated readership for my views. In order to explain what happened when Harriet and

I went to Istanbul that year, I would add that I had in particular written a series of articles in praise of some aspects of the dying Ottoman Empire. In these articles I had made a series of disparaging negative comments about the Committee of Union and Progress, the Turkish nationalist revolutionaries who had come close to overthrowing the centuries-old Sultanate and who had irresponsibly dragged the Ottomans into the fatal decision to enter the Great War.

Frankly I accept that my view of the old Ottoman Empire – in comparison with the nation-states which followed its collapse – is a romantic one which perhaps looks at the past with rose-tinted spectacles. It had already got me into trouble with diaspora Armenians of all kinds, and it has a sort of 'lost causes' aspect to it which equates with a similar nostalgia I have sometimes felt for the multi-national Austrian Empire of the Hapsburgs. But it is worth bearing in mind, when you snigger at those two defunct old Empires, what has followed their demise. Instead of two relatively stable entities, we have, at the time of my writing, fifteen - add them up if you don't believe me - vicious little nation-states, all in deep competition with each other, all ready to indulge in the great twentieth century pastime of ethnic cleansing.

I digress. The one thing that I did not anticipate, however, was that my articles had also upset many Turks. In the course of my writing and in my many despatches, I have of course inevitably referred to the massacres and killing of the Armenian peasantry in Eastern Anatolia during 1915 and the years following. I had avoided the word 'genocide', not out of any fear or lack of conviction but because that word raises issues that go beyond the fact of the killings, which needs to be established first.

When we arrived in Istanbul I found that we had been booked into a fairly smart modern hotel on the Pera side of the city. That very first day I took Harriet down to Sirkeci station. There we got on one of the smart electric trains that now run alongside the Marmara and out to the suburbs. Despite all the electricity, with the doors opening and shutting automatically like the most modern underground system, nevertheless the journey took about the same time as I remembered during the days of the old steam trains of the thirties. My grandfather's large house was in the hills above Makrikoy. Harriet and I got out, as I and my parents always used to, at Cobancesme station just before Makrikoy. Here we went under the railway line and started walking up the long hill.

It was unrecognisable.

I could just see down to the Vali Effendi racecourse between huge blocks of smart flats, but otherwise there were no fields left at all, no break to the lines of high-rise buildings on both sides of the road, which marched steadily right up to the top of the hill. I recognised nothing and when we got to the top there was no sign of where my grandfather's grand house and large garden had been. This is an experience that many in my generation have had. We were one of the first generations to be able to travel extensively. But what has happened is that there have been enormous changes from the time we first began exploring the world. So Istanbul, which, when I used to go there regularly before the war, was a large city of about a million people has turned from just a large city into an enormous megalopolis of eighteen million today. The change is devastating, wherever there were gentle wooded hills, there are now blocks and blocks of high-rise apartments.

But the Galata bridge – ah the Galata bridge - however modernised, is as evocative as ever.

What was most devastating and what I have to face writing about is what happened the next morning. I don't know whether it was a deliberate action by the police, or that it just happened that way – but the following morning Harriet had left early to go to join a friend for a shopping expedition in the now pedestrianised Grande rue du Pera – sorry, the Istiklal Caddesi. I had had a leisurely breakfast and was in the hotel lobby preparatory to going out myself for a spot of sightseeing, when I was accosted by two men, not in uniform. They showed me, well they flashed in front of me, some sort of identification and indicating that they were plain-clothes security officers, said –

"Effendi will you please come with us – a problem has arisen in regard to your travel documents and it is necessary for you to sort it all out at the local police station."

I hesitated, but they then indicated the main swing door of the hotel, and I saw that standing outside were two uniformed policemen, looking in and both clearly waiting for me to come out. In a way this gave me some confidence, as my first thought had been that this was smelling as if it was a hoax or a scam of some sort. I nodded, but said that I wanted to leave a note for my wife with the reception, which I duly did. I then went out with them and into a large car with police markings, which was standing in front of the main entrance.

I appreciate that I am swinging about a bit and not getting on with my narrative in a strict chronological order. Perhaps I am repressing some of the memory. Nevertheless, I have to establish right from the start that I was not traumatised by what followed. In my seven years with the army I have experienced situations potentially more dangerous. Furthermore I have always been able to endure physical pain, though by now being well into my sixties I was not as fit as I had been. Either way, as I was being driven to wherever they wanted me to go I was not any more apprehensive than any journalist or tourist would have been in the circumstances. The police were polite, as Turkish police always have been since Ottoman times, though unwilling or unable to give me any further information about what it was all about.

But the situation changed drastically once I arrived at the local Police station. I found that I had been charged by a lawyer I had never heard of – a certain Kemal Kerinsiz, I think, under Article 301 of the Turkish penal code – a law which had already been in existence since the 1920's. I had vaguely heard about this law, The law makes it a clear criminal offence to "disparage Turkishness'. Heaven knows what this actually means, but in practice it criminalizes any article, speech or writing which 'insults' the Turkish state, or takes any sort of negative line on Turkish history. It is somewhat on the same lines as Pavelic's law making any disparagement of Croat history high treason.

It came as a surprise to me that I had been 'insulting' the modern Turkish state. I have always approved of Ataturk's secular attitude, I welcomed his laws banning the wearing of the veil. I applaud his decision to send his soldiers into the countryside to tear the veils off those peasant women who would not comply. But of course in many of my articles I have referred to the Armenian issue of 1915 and the massacres and deportations which had taken place then. It turned out that it was this which had prompted the charge laid by this nationalist lawyer and which the criminal justice system had to take note of.

I think I remained fairly calm, simply making the usual noises about demanding to have a visit from the British consul. My attitude was, and remains, that I did not feel aggrieved in any way just because I was a British citizen. It may be a ridiculous law, but it was the law of the land. After all, if a Turkish tourist came to England and perpetrated some action that was against the law in the UK, the state had every right to take action against him. When on English soil he was subject to English law, regardless of whether that law was reasonable or not. So, as my possessions were listed, my tie, belt and coat removed, I remained calm, I had been through much worse experiences.

But I was not prepared for the night in the prison to which I was taken outside the city. I had expected to be lodged in a police cell in the district in which I had been arrested. Instead I was driven with a group of other tough, unshaven, men who were part of a batch of arrestees being taken to a large prison on the Asian side. There was no solitary confinement, or single cells. I was thrust into a large communal cell holding about twenty other inmates. I was unceremoniously pushed in, with the words 'Ermeni Giavour' in my ears.

Turks tend to have more respect for the elderly than West Europeans, but it did not unfortunately apply to me in those circumstances. Even now, in my advanced and more tranquil moments of recollection I cannot dwell too long on what happened that night in that ghastly, overcrowded prison cell. I fought back all the time and landed many punches on my assailants, but there was a communal ganging-up against me which eventually overwhelmed me. I did fall asleep in the early hours of the morning as did everyone else. The punches and kicks started again in the morning, but there was no longer the same bile in it and no longer any communal cooperation. My strong reflex attempts to punch back soon put off even those few wishing to continue the beating and I was soon left alone, though

I was unable to get at any of the food which had been pushed through the grille.

At midday the consul arrived together with a fairly high official from the Ministry of Justice. Harriet had of course rushed round to see the consul as soon as she returned from her shopping trip and found my note. She was not let into the prison but waited outside in the consulate car. The consul saw me in a visitor's area and explained about Article 301, and that I simply had to go through the procedure. This was not a government prosecution but one brought by a private individual. The official from the Ministry of Justice sat alongside all the time.. Although I was aching all over, I had protected my face throughout the whole ordeal and there was no outward sign of the beatings that I had endured. I did not of course say a word about what had happened in the night, I knew better than to do that, but I did hint that I might not be able to survive unless I was either bailed – "Impossible at the moment, sir" or I could be transferred to somewhere where I could be in a single cell.

The ministry official nodded, and in fact that very afternoon I was back in a police van and driven back across the high bridge over the Bosporous and into a police station near Taksim, where I was lodged in a small cell, where there was a washbasin and, oh bliss, a loo, rather than just a bucket, in the corner.

I was in that cell for almost a week, waiting, as I am doing now just out of Brixton, to see whether I was going to be prosecuted, in Istanbul under Article 301. It had been made fairly clear that it would be almost impossible to prevent a trial now having to proceed – though in fairness I should add that the general consensus was that I need not worry too much, as the judge was not likely to be sympathetic to the lawyer bringing the case against the express wishes of the authorities. My worry was whether I could at least get out on bail while waiting for the trial on some sort of house arrest. But it was during that week that I spent in this police cell that I went through one of the biggest shocks that I have ever had during the whole of my life.

Chapter 11

Nikko

It was not that I was too self-centred to be interested in the dilemma raised by my mother's wish to die – it was that, as always happened in our family, no one really had any interest in what I thought about it. I will accept that I may well have been a favourite of my mother who always lavished more love on me than she did on either of her daughters, but she never had any respect for any view that I ever advanced. Inevitably if she ever had a problem she would first discuss it with Anne and then ask for William's advice. He would give it forcefully and nothing that I ever said would count for anything – so why should I bother. I am not saying for a moment that William was ever unkind, but he was such a know-all that I always felt a bit inadequate when he was present.

After going through a short period as a Christian at school when I became confirmed like everyone else around me, I began to reject it as I grew older and began to think for myself rather than conforming with all in my peer group. William had become an out-and-out atheist, anti-religious, and profoundly anti-clerical who despised all concepts of spirituality. As far as he was concerned all that mattered was what you could see, touch and feel – everything else was fantasy – self-deception. I am not exaggerating – he did not believe, for instance, that dreams had any significance, or that there was an element in our minds that lie completely outside the material world.

Look, it is not a question of my reacting against him. For heaven's sake I am my own man aren't I – not just an opposite of my elder brother. I do genuinely feel that there is more in life than our mere physical senses perceive. But if I ever talked about these forces – the forces of nature and the forces of the human mind, William would cut me down and his scorn was hurtful. We were a family where we were all encouraged by our father, Conrad, to discuss every topic fully with everyone entitled to their say. However, the flip side of this tolerant encouragement was that the younger ones – me particularly, were squashed by the elders without much parental protection. I was never good at putting forward my own point of view, or in participating in such lively discussions, so I was quickly tied up in knots and put down by William, who delighted in this kind of verbal dominance. It's funny really, if Conrad, who was always fairly strict with us, had ever come across William bullying me with his superior physical strength – not I should hasten to add that he ever did – Conrad would undoubtedly have intervened immediately and William would have been severely punished. But somehow dominance in discussion did not count.

I suppose I must have resented it more than I thought at the time, as I have certainly gone on a bit about it.

It was after I went in my gap year to India and stayed there for several months that I developed an interest in the spirituality, and the religious sensitivity that seems to pervade all life in that country. I became involved in Buddhism and I also saw merit in some aspects of the Hindu way as well. After finishing at University I took to going on spiritual retreats and practising meditation. I had no personal guru, but I became a great lover of Indian music and in particular the Sittar music of Ravi Shankar, whose concerts I have attended in the most unlikely places.

I know that I don't support myself and that I still live in my parent's house. I do work, admittedly for a mere pittance, for a charity devoted to - well I don't really know how exactly to describe it – devoted to nurturing and developing the spiritual well-being of slum dwellers living in the cities of North India. The scorn – no the complete contempt - which my brother pours on this concept does affect me though I try to ignore it. His arguments are always crystal clear. How can I waste my time on being concerned about the morals and belief-systems of people who have little food, no clean drinking water and who are living in material conditions of such squalor. He would usually end with saying something on the lines of –

"For heaven's sake Nikko, get out there and do the little you can to make a small difference for some few people to improve their way of life. They don't care about the existence or non-existence of your God or any God – they care only about the next crust of bread."

Yes – well he was right to a certain extent and I could never reply but stuttered away and left him holding the field. I know I am young for my age and that I am not as mature as William, and I will never be as wise as my Dad, but I do have my own opinions. William is wrong on this point. There is clearly nothing that I or any of my fellow-workers at the charity can possibly significantly do to ameliorate the physical conditions of the children and young people living on the streets in some of these cities. However we can perhaps give some of them some insight into their value as human beings – into the value of the spirit of life, which might perhaps help them more than the extra crust of bread that William wants me to devote my time to.

So what I have to say is that when it came down to it the family were not interested in my view on the matter of euthanasia. Nevertheless I did have a view and I discussed the problem with my Buddhist friends at the

Charity offices. When I first raised the issue, the leader of my group – Joshua - he was not in any way a guru, but he was older than the rest of us, said –

"My dear Nicholas it really is fairly clear, despite the many different branches of Buddhism. In one of the branches ordinary people are required to recite daily a very simple and short statement which simply states – 'I undertake to try and abstain from destroying living beings'. Short simple and concise. So if you accept it, then euthanasia or helping people to commit suicide is wrong. For monks the monastic rule goes even further and I quote – 'Should any monk intentionally deprive, or help to deprive a human being of life, or invite or help him to die, he also is wrong and no longer in communion'. Really it's quite clear."

Well when I heard this it seemed clear enough to me and it did not seem to be all that much different from the Christian attitude. But then I got talking about it with another member of our group, another forceful character – John - whom I love dearly. He pointed out that a vital part of Buddhist teaching is the concept of 'compassion'. Compassion, he said, requires that euthanasia should be acceptable in order to relieve a person who may be suffering from unbearable pain. John went on to take the line that so long as there was no doubt about a sound mind, every man or woman had the right to make up his or her own decision on this point. I assumed that this was likely to be William's position as well, but it turned out I was wrong as it became clear, as the family discussions continued that he was adamantly against help being given to fulfil mother's wishes. John's argument was as clear in an opposite direction as that of our leader. As mother was a sentient human being of sound and capable mind, who had made a clear and irrevocable decision that she wished to end her life,

Buddhist 'compassion' then required that she should be helped to carry that out, and that there is accordingly no moral objection to that help being given.

Oh dear! It appeared that Buddhism looked both ways and offered no clear guidance. After talking it over with John I raised the matter again at one of our group therapy sessions at the end of the working day. There has never been a discussion which aroused such dissension as the one that followed. Our leader – Joshua - usually always so calm, always so ready to see all points of view and rarely to come down one way or another, actually began to lose his cool. After Joshua had again put forward the argument about the sanctity of life, John had raised his point of view about the importance of compassion. In the end, after a lot of unusually heated discussion, Joshua said very firmly that mainstream Buddhist teaching stated unequivocally that ' irrespective of the quality or the nature of a person's motive it is completely immoral; to embark on any course of action designed to destroy or help to destroy a human life'. Such a clear statement was so unusual for him that the actual words have remained clear in my mind'. Joshua's usual answer when these moral dilemma issues arose was to point out inconsistencies in the words – 'good' or 'bad', or the words 'moral' and 'immoral' or the very concept of 'right' and 'wrong'.

I was confused then and I remain confused now. When I asked an Indian friend who used to come with me to Sittar concerts, he didn't help much either by saying that to assist to end a life filled with unbearable pain is surely to perform a 'good' deed and fulfils your moral obligation to that person. But he then went on and on about 'karma' and the inevitable cycle of life and death and back I was as confused as ever. When I tried – and I only tried once – discussing it with William, he told me to stop being so wishy-washy – to pull myself together and as he put it –

"For God's sake, Nikko, make up your own mind based on your own personal experience of life and don't keep on trying to find out what religions or other philosophies might say To be a full human is to make up your own mind on right and wrong and not to have it dictated by someone else."

He is, as always right, but then I quoted to him a few lines from that wonderful thirteenth century Persian poet – Rumi -

This being human is like a guest house.
Every morning a new arrival.
A joy, a depression, a meanness,
some momentary awareness comes
each as an unexpected visitor.

Welcome and entertain them all!
Even if they're a crowd of sorrows,
who violently sweep your house
empty of its furniture,
still treat each guest honorably.
He may be clearing you out
for some new delight.

The dark thought, the shame, the malice,
meet them at the door laughing,
and invite them in.
Be grateful for whoever comes,
because each has been sent
as a guide from beyond.

William stared at me as I finished. I had not expected that he would even have heard me out, and let me finish. But oh God he was moved – my strong materialist elder brother was moved – moved – by something I had said.

Then he laughed, albeit a trifle uneasily and said –

"That's good – brother – that's good, whoever this Rumi guy is. But in the end it doesn't actually help us one way or another does it. Like all philosophers or religious gurus, they come out with deep and meaningful phrases at which we all nod our heads, but when it comes down to it they don't help us decide on what is the best way to proceed in any practical problem."

He smiled at me as if I was still a child. I said nothing, but I was clear that I disagreed with him. These so-called deep meaningful phrases can sometimes help.

Chapter 12

Conrad

The relief of being away from that ghastly communal prison cell was such that somehow all the fears, inherent in the actual situation I was in, seemed to evaporate. I really could not believe that I was in any real danger. It is true that in the many articles that I had written over the years – and particularly those emanating from one of the many ethnic cleansing situations that I have had to cover – I had often referred to the Armenian massacres of eighty years ago, as being the start of the cycle of these events that have so disgraced the twentieth century. But I would contend that I have done so in a fairly cool and purely historical context. I cannot recall ever having used the word 'genocide' in any of my articles in reference to any of the twentieth century horrors we have gone through. I have however often used the phrase 'ethnic cleansing' in all these cases.

After I had been taken out of the large communal cell in the prison on the Asian side and let into my new cell I suddenly realised that I was very hungry. I had not eaten anything since breakfast at the hotel the day before. I knew no Turkish, but I am a natural linguist, and I soon got the attention of a policeman who would pass down the corridor outside my cell. I rubbed my tummy and said the words for food and water. I also offered some money for the purchase. The money was politely rejected, though the man nodded. About half an hour later the door was opened and a tray with some hot food on a plate, together with a large mug of weak tea without milk was brought in by the same man and placed on the bed beside me.

I should make the contrast clear. This was a cell in a police station that I was now in and the men on duty were all policemen not prison guards. Turkish policemen have always been very correct and polite – a throwback to Ottoman times when their reputation for formal courtesy was streets ahead of any other European Empire. I should add that the food was surprisingly tasty, though this might have been the effect of my being ravenously hungry.

I slept well that night and indeed on each of the four further nights that I slept in that cell. I seem to be forever fated to waiting to see if I am going to be charged with some criminal offence. But I did not feel like a criminal then, just as I don't feel like one now. There is however a difference. In Istanbul waiting to be charged under Article 301, I never for one moment ever believed that the law under which I was languishing in prison was either just or reasonable in any way whatsoever. It was not only that I felt no guilt or shame at my predicament, but I remained always quite certain that the law as it stood was unjust and unreasonable. Furthermore it was clearly a retrograde law that was likely to cause a lot of difficulty in any attempt by Turkey to join the Common Market. In Istanbul, therefore, I was in a state of anger at the authorities, and this anger helped in keeping me steady and ready to face all eventualities. My current situation is different. Whilst I have no doubts at all about my own moral position in deciding to help my wife to get what she desperately wanted, I do not have that same certainty about the justice or reasonableness of the Suicide Act, as I had about the ridiculous Article 301.

I accept that Society needs to take a stand of one kind or another on the issue of citizens killing themselves, or wishing to do so. It is so obviously a situation that could be open to the most terrible abuse that Society must seek to regulate it. So, as I sit here waiting for the CPS to make up its mind, whilst I am anxious about how my own actions might be viewed, I am not in the least bit outraged that a law exists which makes those actions criminal.

Imprisonment in a foreign prison where you can't speak the language of your guards can be a very frightening experience. However in my case there were two factors in operation which had the effect of reducing any possible trauma. Firstly my experience on that first night was such that ending up on my own in this solitary cell was a great relief. Secondly Harriet was nearby, working tirelessly at the consulate and visiting my prison daily. She regularly brought in the most delicious food which I shared with the polite young policeman, who himself frequently brought me mugs of that refreshing weak Turkish tea.

So, I can't put it off any longer – I must come to the moment in my life when I was faced with an extraordinary revelation about myself.

It was I think on the third day, fairly early in the morning, that my door was opened and my same friendly jailor came in and told me that I had a visitor. Harriet had been allowed regularly to bring me food, but she had never been allowed down into the cells – and this being a police station not a prison, there were no facilities for visitors to come and see prisoners. The consul had of course been allowed to come down and see me in my cell to report on what was happening, but apart from him I had had no visitors and indeed did not expect any.

To my astonishment, after making his announcement, Hamid brought in a small armchair and placed it, facing my bed on which I was sitting, in the narrow area between the bed and the wall. I am not entirely sure how the name Hamid is spelt but that was what it sounded like, and we had by now become sufficiently friendly for me not to have to refer to him as 'my jailor' any longer. His attitude was one of great deference towards whoever was about to come in, and I wondered whether I was about to be interrogated by some Judge or high official of the Ministry of Justice. The door had remained open while all this was going on, but I remained seated on the bed the only other piece of furniture in the room. Hamid returned immediately after he had placed the armchair and bowed in a little old lady.

His deference towards her showed that whoever she was, she was clearly somebody of some influence and standing. I had of course immediately stood up on the entrance of a lady, but the cell was small and what with the basin and loo at the end and now the armchair there was not much room. The lady stood staring at me without a smile or any expression on her face. She did not look down but began pulling off her fine lace gloves, still staring silently at me. She looked very chic and was expensively dressed – but her face was wizened with wrinkles and age-spots. I was never ever completely sure what age she was, but she must have been in her early nineties.

Hamid was at a loss at the silence as I stood waiting for whatever it was that this was all about. He shuffled a bit and then said nodding at me,

"Conrad Bridgeman effendi – madam,"

Then turning to me and indicating again with a sort of nod at the lady still standing bolt upright beside him, he said,

"Doctor Yasmin Kemal hanum".

He then managed to shuffle forward and pull back

the chair for the lady to sit. He then motioned me to sit back on the bed on which I had been sitting for two days. However this was as it were my cell, my home ground, and in a sort of stubborn and rather pointless emphasis of that, I remained standing. I felt the necessity of offering something to this visitor as if she was a guest. I leant back and offered her a plate of biscuits that Harriet had left for me the previous day. The lady smiled for the first time, declined the offer and then said a sentence or two to Hamid. I did not understand her words, but they were clearly thanks – and dismissal. Hamid bowed again and went out, closing and locking the door behind him. Meanwhile – ridiculous male honour satisfied - I finally sat down.

I have no difficulty whatsoever in recalling and being able to set down accurately the conversation which then took place between us. There may have been gaps, exclamations and all sorts of interruptions in the course of the conversation, but other than that I have set out exactly what was said. As a matter of fact it consisted mostly of a monologue from the old lady – I said very little myself. As she spoke she did pick at the plateful of 'leblebi' nuts which I had been able to dig out of the little cupboard by the side of my bed after the biscuits were rejected.

In order to make the position clear I should explain that my arrest had not gone unnoticed in Istanbul, nor for that matter in the world outside Turkey. The lawyer who had laid the charge was notorious in his pursuit of writers and journalists whom he believed had contravened Article 301 – but this was the first time that he had invoked it against a foreigner who happened to be visiting the country. The name of 'Conrad Bridgemen effendi' was accordingly all over the newspapers. But it went further than that. The editor of my own employing newspaper had fairly quickly decided that a very public media campaign would be useful and the British Consul had agreed that the more publicity there was the better my chances of at least being released under what they called house arrest. Furthermore it was not just my own newspaper that started running the story. The arrest of a British citizen and a journalist of some standing under this controversial law, inevitably became an issue which was on the point of turning into an international incident. The Turkish government was clearly embarrassed, but a nationalist backlash was making it impossible for the government to be appearing to bow to Western pressure. So it was that my imprisonment was common knowledge.

The old lady, however, made no attempt to explain how she had come to learn about my predicament. I should add that her English was excellent, though she spoke with that slight American accent which was usual with Turkish speakers of the language. The old lady spoke firmly throughout and it was soon clear to me that she had thought out exactly what she was going to say and how she was going to say it.

"My name is Yasmin, Mr. Bridgeman. I am a well-known Doctor of some standing in the city, though I am no longer in practice. I became a doctor and chose it as my profession almost entirely due to the short friend-ship that I developed with your mother – Olga – when I was 16."

Well, inevitably, with this mention of my mother, who I knew was born in Constantinople and was married to my father at the grand British embassy, now a mere consulate, my interest quickened and I stopped simply wondering what it was all about.

"My mother, madam?"

"Certainly. Your mother was Olga Avakian was she not?"

"Yes, of course."

"Well, you obviously don't know about it, but before your mother met your father she was deeply in love with my brother – Selim. They met while she was in the girls section of Robert College and he was in the boys section. Your mother couldn't have been much more than seventeen at the time. I'm not sure whether you can understand, but for an Armenian girl and a Turkish boy to be in love in the Constantinople of 1915 was a completely and utterly impossible situation. Believe me it was far more difficult for them than it ever could have been for Romeo and Juliet. Your mother's and my brother's love was quite impossible and eventually they each went their separate ways. He joined the army and went to the war against the British Indian army in Mesopotamia, she became a nurse and worked at the Turkish hospital in Uskudar."

"Uskudar," I said, "that's on the Asian side isn't it?"

"Yes. It is a famous hospital – I am one of the governors as it happens. I think the British called it Scutari. It was where Florence Nightingale practised during the Crimean War."

I knew of course that my mother had been a nurse and had worked in several hospitals. However she had only ever spoken about her work in the Imperial Ottoman Hospital in Smyrna, where she had been when she met my father after the great fire. At this point I was still in the dark as to where all this was leading – but I was now totally involved in the narrative. The prison walls seemed to recede, and we were afloat in the story of my mother and her life as a young woman. I suppose I may have looked eager at a further silence, for she then said –

"We have a lot of time, Mr. Bridgeman, and you anyway are not going anywhere and I too have all day..

However I suppose I must begin to cut this a bit short. What happened was that Selim was badly wounded at the front and was sent back to the hospital in which Olga was working. Your mother looked after him. Eventually she then called on me and my mother to let us know that he was now back in Constantinople. The army administration was not very efficient in those days and we had no idea what had happened to him. My mother and I began visiting him regularly. I was only 14 – your mother was five years older than me but she befriended me and would take me with her when she went on her round of the wards, whilst my mother sat with Selim. I adored Olga and it was as a result of those afternoons with her that I decided to become a doctor myself."

At this point the old lady folded her hands in her lap and sat contemplating for a minute or two. I had nothing to say, and in view of her earlier comment I was careful not to appear impatient. But fascinating as all this was, it was only history, and it did not seem to amount to much more than the nostalgic memory of an old woman rambling about her past. But then she resumed –

"They fell in love all over again – though in a way they had never really fallen out of love. My brother was now – wait a moment I can't exactly recall but he would have been about 22, while Olga was I suppose 19. However, once again it remained as impossible as it had been two years previously. In fact now even worse in view of the unfortunate deaths of the Armenians of the interior that had taken place meanwhile. I recall several occasions when Olga tried to approach my mother – but she was bitterly anti-Armenian. Her husband – my father Nazim - also a doctor, had been shot by the Armenian rebels during the siege of Van, and she poured out all her anger and her frustrations onto poor Olga. I myself was only a young girl, but I was present at several unpleasant scenes between them."

There was another long pause.

"Some of what I am now going to tell you I have had to work out for myself as obviously I was not present. All I can tell you for certain is that your mother Olga and my brother Selim met again in 1921/22 in Smyrna during the period of the Greek administration. Olga was employed at the Imperial Ottoman Hospital, and also at the Armenian Hospital in the city – three days at the one and three days at the other. I myself never knew exactly what Selim was doing there – but it must have been something clandestine as he was at the time an officer in the Turkish nationalist army – and this was a city under Greek control. But what I do know, as Olga herself told me, is that once they met, now for the third time, they began living together in a house they had rented, as man and wife."

"Well then came the catastrophic and total defeat of the Greeks followed by the entry of the triumphant Turkish army into the town. This was followed by the great fire which consumed the city – and consumed my brother who died in the flames. Olga escaped and eventually got back to Constantinople, brought back I think by your father. Yes, yes I'm sure you have heard all about it – and no, I will not go into any question of how the fire started – its all a long time ago, and we are not likely to agree are we."

"After getting back to her family in Constantinople, Olga came one day to visit my mother. I was not at home when she arrived, but I came in just after. She was already speaking to my mother in the sitting room telling her all that had happened. I did not disturb them, but stood in the hall listening. She told my mother how she and Selim had lived together for nearly a year, then what had happened at the end in the great fire, and then told her that she herself was now almost two months pregnant, and that the baby she was carrying was my mother's grandchild – the only grandchild she would ever have as it happens – the offspring of her son Selim."

I was now totally involved in the old lady's story, but strange to say I still did not see what should have now become obvious. I suppose I was still looking puzzled, because Yasmin – I can't really keep saying the old lady anymore – gave an exasperated sigh and raising her voice she said –

"Olga had her baby – it was born in London nine months later on the day of the signing of the Treaty of Lausanne, supposedly born premature, seven months after she married Harry Bridgeman, which marriage, held at the old British Embassy I attended as a guest. For God's sake man – don't look as if you don't understand what I am telling you – you, sir, are my biological nephew, the grandchild my mother claimed she never had. For Olga had blurted it all out to my mother, imagining I suppose that the existence of a blood grandchild might bring some solace to the poor woman. But not a bit of, not a bit of it! With enormous passion and vehemence my mother ordered Olga out of the house, telling her that she never wanted to see her ever again. As Olga stumbled away in tears to the front door, my mother came out and her voice rising to a shriek she solemnly cursed your mother - my friend, my brother's lover, and the mother of my nephew and my mother's grandchild, her only grandchild - wishing her and the baby she was carrying, ill for the rest of her life. I of course had melted away into the kitchen so as not to be seen to have witnessed what had taken place. I did not however give up my friendship with Olga and spoke to her many times and was present at her wedding to Harry at the old British Embassy a few weeks later."

I was now speechless. I could not take it all in. At that moment I still had not thought of what it might all mean for me. My only thought was for my Dad. After yet another silence as Yasmin stared at me, I finally said –

"And my Dad – what about my Dad."

"Come sir – he knew, of course he knew. You must know your mother's honourable character, she would never have played a trick like that on Harry or any man for that matter. She told him she was pregnant from Selim before he even proposed to her. When she told him everything he accepted that he would become the father of the boy or girl that was not his own biological child. He loved your mother….and he has been a good father to you hasn't he."

I was in my sixties – I was as mature as I would ever become, but at that moment in that prison cell as my mind turned to my Dad – I began to weep. I wept silent tears that flooded my eyes as I thought of all the days I had spent with my father, my beloved father, who had given me so much in my life, and who had given it to me even though it now seems that he had always known that I was not his child but the offspring of another.

The old lady – yes for in the end that was all she was – did not get up, nor did she lean forward or in any way try to comfort me. She did not extend a hand or try to stem the silent flow of tears, but just sat looking down at her folded hands. After all I was a man in my sixties and she was over ninety. There were no children or young persons here who had to be guided or comforted, just two elderly people contemplating the past. We sat like that for over twenty minutes as my grief and love for my Dad, the only Dad I ever knew, poured out of me.

As Yasmin saw that my grief was ending, she rose and

knocked on the door. Hamid must have been right out-side as the door opened immediately despite the very light knock. At the door she turned back and smiled at me. We did not say a further word to each other.

Chapter 13

Conradin

I know that I am only 15, but that doesn't mean that I don't have my own ideas about what is right and wrong. Religious instruction started at the Catholic boarding school to which my mother had insisted I should go, from the moment I first arrived there at the age of 12. I soaked it all up and followed with certainty all I was being taught – and why not. The friars were all good men and at 13 you are easily influenced by people who you know in your heart are good men and who clearly have your interest at heart.

But 13 becomes 14 and then 15 and I became more guarded, less innocent perhaps. The event which forced me to start thinking for myself happened just after my fourteenth birthday. Of course since getting confirmed we were all encouraged to go to Confession regularly. This was not taken by any of our resident teachers. Priests from outside would call to take confession in the school chapel for those boys needing it.

As it happens this business of private confession was a part of the institutional belief system that I had found the most unsatisfactory and difficult to follow. Oddly enough whenever I talked these things over with my Grandpa Conrad, although I knew that he was not a believer, this was the part of Catholic teaching which to my surprise he found the most satisfying and reasonable. I don't know what my Dad might have felt as I knew better than to talk it over with him.

Anyway, the old Priest who used to come to take our confessions scarcely seemed even to listen, and if I talked too much he would indicate that he had heard enough, gave me whatever penance he thought appropriate and then absolved and blessed me. Then out I went, to be followed immediately by another 13 year old boy like a factory assembly line. On the particular occasion which caused me so much distress the Priest taking confession was not the same old man I had been used to, but another younger man whom I had not seen before who was standing in for our usual priest.

I knelt and came out with my wretched little boy sins and a confession of what I had done in bed in the dormitory a few nights before. Instead of yawning and asking me if I was repentant and urging me to fight the habit and then passing on, this priest kept asking me what I had been thinking of, what had been my thoughts, what were the details. It was not that I got confused, I just felt a sort of deep shame at the priest's persistence in trying to get out of me details of the thoughts that had been in my mind during my shabby and shameful act. My Dad may be a pompous old fool but he has taught me to act courageously if I believed anything was wrong, even if it were to cost me later. I knew something here was wrong and I knew that I would probably end up being punished, but I felt that I could not sit anymore in that wretched cubicle trying to sort out what I should be saying. I simply slithered out through the curtain, nodded at the next boy in line and went back to the study which I shared with two friends.

As it happened my fear of being punished was groundless. No one ever said anything about my leaving the confession box abruptly and a couple of weeks later the old priest returned. But I never got back into the habit of going to confession. Of course I never said a word to anyone, least of all to my Dad whom I thought would have sort of rejoiced and said something like 'I told you so...' Well... no...perhaps not! Now I come to think about it, if he saw my distress I think, to be fair, he would not have rubbed it in.

After the end of the summer holidays in that year 1999, I went back to school and the issue that was obsessing the rest of the family was no longer part of my life. However, I had not forgotten the passionate words of my grandmother as she was wheeled out of my Auntie Ann's sitting room. My school may have been a bit of an old-fashioned English public school, but it was well-run and we were encouraged to think about moral issues and to discuss any problem we might have with one of the brothers who had been designated as our moral tutor.

I had received a letter from my mother who in passing said that discussions were still going on around my grandmother's wish to go to Switzerland to die. Angela had said no more than that, but I could read between the lines and I knew well that she was horrified. I don't think that my mum got on well with Harriet. However I have read enough novels now to know that relations between women and their mothers-in-law are notoriously difficult – though I must say that I have never seen any reason why people could not get on with grandma. She was always good to me, treating me seriously. I liked her.

Nevertheless after that letter I felt that I ought to find out what the Church to which I now belonged – of my own free will whatever Dad might say – believed on the issue of Euthanasia. Without disclosing the personal reasons behind my request for guidance, I raised the matter of euthanasia with my moral tutor at our monthly private tutorial sessions. His answer was very clear – completely unequivocal – and without any ifs or buts. It comforted me at the time and I ceased then to be at all confused. But later... At that tutorial we discussed it fully but his final words were –

"My son, the teaching of the Roman Catholic Church is very clear and brooks for no confusion, contradiction or weasel words of compromise. It totally condemns euthanasia as a 'crime against life', and what is worse a 'crime against God'."

When I asked why it was a crime against God, he explained to me that we must all believe not only in the existence of God, but also in His essential goodness in his plan for mankind. I think he used another word rather than 'goodness', but that is what I understood. Accordingly, he had gone on to say, if that is so, then 'Despair' – I do remember that that is exactly the word he used – is a terrible sin because it postulates that you no longer believe in the God of love and compassion, who orders all things for the good of mankind. I muttered something about free will and the human need also to exercise compassion, but he dismissed that easily and as soon as I raised it I felt that I was parroting my father – and that I was determined not to do.

Anyway I really liked my tutor. I felt instinctively that he was a good man – and good men don't lead others astray do they. After this meeting he leant me two books. One was a fairly short one on the Nazi's Euthanasia programme of the late thirties, which had aroused the only really strong Roman Catholic opposition to that odious regime. The other, by some American professor, was on the ethics and the danger of an enforced sterilisation programme. After reading these, or at least as much as I could stomach, at our next tutorial I raised the question which had arisen for me. How was the Nazi euthanasia project, or ideas about sterilising people who were unhealthy relevant to the issue I had originally raised? My original problem was regarding a single person who was gravely ill and suffering badly and who himself wanted to end his life. No one was forcing anybody to die. The answer came immediately, without any hesitation and settled my doubts on this matter, which no longer troubled me for the rest of the term. He said –

"But Conradin I gave you these books to show you what happens when you first start to allow the thought of 'assisted suicide' to take hold in society. Those books I lent you show you where it will lead to in the end. First genuine compassion starts to relax the rules, but then one by one you slide down the slope to – death by arrangement – and finally to death just for social convenience."

My tutor went on to point out how once you permit voluntary assisted suicide in any society it will inevitably lead in the end to that society accepting non-voluntary euthanasia, allowing the killing, which they will no doubt call 'kulling' of selected members of the population.

"Beware Conradin, beware the capacity to evil of mankind. You saw where it led to in Nazi Germany and don't think for a minute that it could not happen again."

I did see it and I accepted what he said completely. He was right wasn't he! I came away at least being completely clear what my Church required me to believe, even if I still had just a few reservations at the back of my mind. At 15 years old I accepted every word. As I was no longer in any confusion on the issue I put it right out of my mind for the rest of the term. That particular term was a great revelation for me in all sorts of ways. My voice had fully broken and to my joy it turned out that I had a good clear tenor voice. I joined the school choir and I found a great delight in learning to read music and to partake in that special pleasure of making music together.

In academic matters I was already fond of History as

a school subject – it was undoubtedly my best subject. By the end of this term I had decided to take history as my major subject for my entry into the Sixth form next year.

I was naturally pretty good at sports and I became the school Squash champion and captained the school Squash team when we went to play against other schools. I was full of myself, and why not. I was happy and had few hang-ups either in myself or in reference to my friends – boys and girls.

I went home for the Xmas holidays of that year feeling great in myself and no longer giving a single thought to poor Grandma's situation. But within days of getting home the crisis in the family began to come to a climax – and all the certainties I had achieved during the term evaporated.

Chapter 14

Conrad

I stayed in that police cell only for a further two days. Neither the British Consul in Istanbul, nor my editor back in the UK sending off flurries of outraged texts, nor the Foreign Office, had been able to do much except to raise a lot of publicity. Actually, I myself had some sympathy with the Turkish authorities. We in the West go on and on about the importance in any society of the rule of law – but the moment one of our citizens get caught in the coils of that law in a developing country, we complain and the media bleats and screams. Of course it was and it remains a totally ridiculous law – but it was the law and very openly so. If the law allows a private prosecution of a criminal offence, then it was a situation that had to be faced.

But where all the official channels had failed, Doctor Yasmin, one of the governors of the great Uskudar Hospital and with all the respect and goodwill that she had at her disposal, succeeded. I have no idea how she did it, but I believe that the very next day after she had left me she went to see the lawyer who had brought the private prosecution and this KK had then quite voluntarily withdrawn the charges. The case was closed and I was released. Harriet's comment as I came out of that police station was –

"My God Conrad darling you look fit – being under arrest must suit you. A bit pale, but you've lost weight - where's your beer belly gone."

We were euphoric. Of course I never said a word to her or to anyone else as to that first night in the prison on the Asian side. My editor texted me to suggest that

I stayed on for a few days and have a holiday, trying to make it appear as if he was being ultra-generous. The cynical old bastard! My predicament had been newsworthy, and as he had had the monopoly of the news stories he was determined to milk it further – and of course holiday or not I had to send him a couple more articles.

But it is true that Harriet and I had not really had a holiday together - just the two of us without any children - for many years. I think that we had the best week together since our honeymoon. Certainly I look back on it as our last carefree days together before the start of Harriet's illnesses which were to blight our last years. We left the plush but rather soulless chain hotel the newspaper had put us in on the Pera side and moved into a little family-run hotel in the SultanAhmet district on the Stamboul side.

Of course I introduced Harriet to Yasmin and we visited her several times and we took her out to dinner. But I must add that I never told Harriet what I had learnt from her. Furthermore the good lady doctor herself never once alluded to my paternity again, even when no one else was present. On that day of revelation in the police cell, I had after fifteen minutes finally ended my sobbing at the thought of my kind, calm, upright, loving father. Yasmin had then stood and bending forward she had held my hand between her two hands and kissed me long and lingeringly on my forehead. I remained head down. I was still in an emotional state trying to absorb all the implications of what I had just heard. Without looking up I said –

"A man who had so loved his wife that he had looked after me as his son all his life, without a word to anyone."

Yasmin took my head between her hands and said -

"Conrad, my son, don't think like that for a moment. Look, you remember how you and your whole family used to come here for your summer holidays when you were young. Well I would see your mother during those visits– and you and your little brother – and your father. He loved you – he loved you, Conrad – he loved you for yourself, I saw it, I knew it. Come sir, you're far too old to succumb now to such a thought about your father."

Turning she leant over the armchair and knocked on the door. The door opened immediately and there stood Hamid. Yasmin smiled at him and then turned again and extended her hand for a handshake. I couldn't deal with the emotions boiling up in me with a simple handshake. I stood up and leaning somewhat clumsily over the armchair I took her outstretched hand in both mine and raised it to my lips and held it there squeezing hard.. The old lady with a grace and with a slightly amused smile finally pulled away and walked out, followed by a very deferential Hamid, without another word.

At the end of our week holiday we had to return home, and once back in London the ordinary pressures of everyday life started again. Both Anne and William were married and had had children but Sima and Nikko were still living with us. My assignment to the disintegrating Yugoslavia was still open and in due course I went off for my final days there. But before all this started, before I left Istanbul, I had to come to terms with what I had been told by Yasmin. So it was that before leaving the city I paid one last call on her at her flat, but without taking Harriet who went off to get her hair done and do some last minute shopping for the grandchildren.

After drinking the excellent Turkish coffee served by her maid or carer or whatever, I told her that I had come to say goodbye. It was clear between us that in the circumstances this was likely to be our last ever meeting. Yasmin never said a word – just nodded. But at that point I took the plunge and asked if she could tell me a bit about her brother. I also asked whether she knew anything more about those days he spent with my mother in Smyrna, where presumably I was conceived before the great fire. Yasmin stayed silent for some time, then still sitting upright with her wizened old hands in her lap, she began speaking in a rather flat tired voice. At first she talked about her own father – that would be my biological grandfather – who had himself been a doctor. She recounted what she knew about his death, shot by Armenian insurgents during the Siege of Van. She spoke about the deep and everlasting hatred which her mother had felt for Olga, my mother, her son's lover. Then, movingly, though still with the flat tired voice, she at last came to speak about her brother – Selim – my biological father. She made his character come to life though it was all more than seventy years ago.

At last she finished. She was clearly exhausted and now for the first time in our relationship she was herself moved and no longer the dried-up somewhat emotionless old lady who had originally entered my prison cell. She rose and went out of the room, coming back fairly quickly with two photos. They were both small box-camera type photographs, old but surprisingly not faded. One was a photo of Selim, my biological father – a young man, in this photo, scarcely even 20 years old. He had a penetrating look with black eyes, handsome, dark, with a thick moustache but otherwise clean-shaven, which even I could recognise as very much the fashion for young Turkish men of the time. Despite the serious posed style of the old photo I seemed to see a lovely secret smile – or was that just me? The second photo had clearly been taken in a hospital. It showed the same young man, a little older and without the moustache, When I studied it carefully with a magnifying glass later I saw that he was looking pale and haggard and he seemed to have lost his left arm. Sitting on the other side of the bed and holding his right hand tight was a stunningly beautiful absolutely radiant woman, no young girl but certainly still a teenager. It was my mother.

I don't think that either of us said another word. I pocketed the photos – kissed her on her wrinkled cheeks and left. I never ever saw her again.

So that old rascal Stavros had been completely wrong when he used to tease me about my English genes. There never were any! It turns out, after all, that it was my volatile emotional younger brother Billy who had the English genes and who was genuinely half-Armenian and half-English, not me. I am genetically half Armenian and half Turkish. I'm afraid that this was not all that unusual in the turbulent period during and just after the great War; but in my case it was the result of an equal and loving union, not the rape and marriage forced on some young girls during those terrible events of the death marches of Armenians, whose deportation was decreed by Talaat and the Young Turk government of 1915. What difference did this new knowledge make to me?

I am tempted to say none at all. Certainly I can be absolutely certain that it made not a whit of difference to my feelings for my father. If anything the love and respect that I had always had for the British naval officer who had been my role-model, my Dad, my friend all my life, was if anything enhanced by the knowledge that he had always known that I was not his biological offspring. Even as he lay dying and I held his hand telling him of the real circumstances of the death of my brother Billy – his only biological son – he still never said a word to me about what he had always known. Perhaps by the end, at a certain level he was no longer even aware of it.

So that aspect – that memory of my Dad – did not waver one little bit. On the other hand my view about my own identity did begin to change. I recall having put to someone the situation of the baby son of deceased English missionaries, brought up entirely within and part of a Chinese family. Chinese identity of course – but would there be something of his English genes, particularly if in later life he learned of his ancestry? Was not this somewhat like my own situation? I had always been a little obsessed with identity as a result of my own 'half and half' background – and now it had become even more complicated.

As I studied the two photos minutely later, I could see the clear resemblance between my own features and the secretly smiling young man with the serious pose. So this was where my dark eyes and straight black hair came from. Of course I remained as English as I had always been. After all I had been educated at an English public school; I had served for seven years in the British army; all my attitudes, all my prejudices were as English as those of all my friends and peers. In a way Stavros had been right – even if wrong about the actual genes. Nevertheless the Chinese missionary example haunted me. There was something…. something.

As a family, even with a traditional naval officer father, we were always perhaps a bit more ebullient and prone to hugging and kissing in a way that my English friends in the twenties and thirties were not. It was ironic for me to reflect that my irrepressible younger brother Billy – who really was half-English – was always more volatile and emotional than I, and that it was I, with no

English genetic make-up at all who was teased as being the most un-Armenian of the family. I suppose it just goes to show how pointless ideas of racial characteristics, blood-lines and genetic inheritance are. Doesn't it all go to prove that it is all a matter of education and upbringing? Those enlightenment philosophers of the eighteenth century were right. If you could bring up from birth a group of children, all from different backgrounds and nationalities, on a desert island right from the start – they would all end up being Islanders and not Serbs or Croats, or Turks or Armenians. Nationalism of all kinds is entirely taught and manipulated by others and has nothing whatsoever to do with genes.

But is all that quite right? I have always been a bit obsessed with personal identity. I spent hours discussing it with my friend Mardik, both when I was stationed in Cairo and also on one memorable occasion sitting in the hills of Moab overlooking the river Jordan, where on a picnic we had been joined by two local little Arab boys with startlingly blue eyes and fair blond hair. Perhaps that obsession had some basis in some sort of atavistic understanding that there was something unusual in my own genetic make-up.. Oh dear – no, no, that is to think a bit like Nikko with all that stuff about 'life forces' and 'karma' and the 'inner self'". I may not be as contemptuous about all that as William, but I have certainly inherited enough from my Avakian grandfather to reject all that mystic stuff.

In the end there is a limit to how long you can ponder about these matters. You have to 'get on with it' as my commanding officer used to say. But what the disclosure in Istanbul did do to me was to make me think for the first time for many years a little more about the Armenian side of my character. Since those days before the War when I used to take my holidays as a boy in

Bolis (Istanbul) with the Avakians and all the rest of our extended family, I had neglected this aspect of my make-up. You get busy, leave school and go into the army – you start a career – you marry – you have children – you bring them up. You establish your position in society through your work, and all those other issues about your parents and your childhood and your identity fade away.

But then suddenly it's all over. The children have grown up and have left and are establishing their own life. You are suddenly old and no longer have a job or the need for a public persona. Then you find that the memory of all those busy years of work and establishment begin to fade and all of a sudden your memory is full of the days before your twenties. Those issues of identity and who you are and where you came from begin to arise all over again. It was when I got back from my last assignment in Yugoslavia, when it was made clear that it was time I retired and that I would not be getting another post anywhere, that I decided that I would at last make a voyage to Armenia itself, to see if going there, would help in any way as to my issues of identity. Harriet had not then had her first stroke but it was clear that she was not well enough to come. I planned to be away only a few weeks.

But before that I had my last assignment to Yugoslavia to complete.

Chapter 15

Conrad

After the extraordinary events that took place during those few weeks that I spent in Istanbul, I was
required to finish my original assignment to the disintegrating Yugoslavia. We both returned from Turkey and
I then travelled out, leaving Harriet at home. This time
I decided to stay in Belgrade. My despatches home on
this second time round were not popular. The Anglo-
Saxon public love to have a current hate figure and Milosevic fitted the bill perfectly. Not that I had any time
for him myself, but I tended to report on the many Serbs
I met, who were as fed up with him as any of his critics
abroad. It didn't help that I also reported on the many
Croats I met who were as disillusioned with the ranting
Tudjman. But the Western media on the whole continued to insist that what was at stake was the "continual
ethnic hatreds of these benighted Balkan peoples".

There has already been an enormous amount of literature outlining the details of the wars that broke out in
the former Yugoslavia. Serbs and Croats fighting each
other in the Krajina, and in fits and starts throughout
Bosnia; Croats and Bosnian Muslims viciously slaugh-
tering each other in and around Mostar, after the ending of their original arrangement; Serbs relentlessly
bombarding Bosnian Muslims in Sarajevo. I re-read
them all and I become more confused as I sit waiting
for the CPS to make up its mind on the assisted suicide
of Harriet. I find that in retrospect I am no longer as
clear about these events as I was when I covered them.
I re-read my own articles written at the time – and I try
to reconcile them with all the books and essays pouring

out from participants from all sides.

But my memory itself is not confused. It stays very clear particularly in respect to the many mixed-marriage couples I met who extended to me all that traditional Balkan hospitality which all the different ethnic groups fully shared. Serbo-Croat couples forced apart, or struggling to keep their children from succumbing to the pressures of the nationalist propaganda being directed against them from Zagreb and Belgrade.

It was a problem that all the different communities, who supposedly hated each other, shared. It was maddening to watch how the different diasporas – those who had made it out of the country and lived comfortable lives – Croats in the USA and England - Bosnian Muslims in Germany – Serbs everywhere - drove the nationalist agenda onto their compatriots struggling to live a reasonable life in the land in which they were born. I should have been less agitated, for surely as we grow older we are supposed to become calmer and wiser – but this did not seem to apply to me. I was well into my sixties when I was covering Yugoslavia, yet I was becoming more excitable, more angry at what I saw as injustice and this prejudice was coming out in my articles.

I will digress here – oh no not again I hear – but it is a helpful comment. It was my youngest daughter Sima who recently pointed out to me the different reactions I appear to have had towards the horrors and the genocide that took place in Ruanda, compared with the problems and ethnic cleansing that took place during the wars in Yugoslavia. It did leave me feeling a little guilty. I had to admit to myself, as I think back, that I must have viewed – and to my shame I think I still do – the Ruandan tragedy as something peculiarly African. My Editor used to call out at the conferences held in his office when we decided who was to cover what in the developing news-

"Africa is a basket case and has been right from the start. I'm not going to waste resources sending people there. New political ideas or developments are not going to come from there."

We journalists tended to agree and I suppose none of us wanted to be the ones posted there. There must be an element of European elitism in me – though heaven knows I did get upset when I saw the first pictures of the Hutu-Tutsi horrors as they first appeared.

But what was so very sad about the former Yugoslavia was the way it so suddenly fell apart in conflicts and deaths when it had been a state that under Tito and for a short time after, had achieved stability, and had had the capacity of getting many different people with vastly different histories to live together. It had encompassed the existence of social circumstances which could and did lead to stable and happy mixed marriages between these different communities.

In contrast to this – never mind the Africa/Europe difference – Ruanda as a post-colonial; state had never really achieved that sort of stability. The Hutu-Tutsi history of dominance and enslavement was quite different and no synthesis had ever been achieved. Whereas the disintegration of Yugoslavia was the collapse of a state, which despite its several faults had nevertheless given the majority of its citizens the ability to live in some harmony with each other.

When you consider what mainstream Europeans happily did to each other during the first half of the Twentieth Century – one is surprised at how they can stand on their pedestal of moral superiority and condemn the people of south-eastern Europe as primitive Balkan peasants. Certainly these Balkan people were manipulated by unscrupulous leaders into believing that they could no longer live under a representative federal government – even though they had been doing so for more than forty years. The propaganda emanating from their respective diasporas and from their odious and devious leaders slowly but surely drove them more and more apart.

The charge, emanating particularly from the West, trumpets the accusation - 'Ah well they are all basically primitives, who have hated each other for centuries, without our civilised values.' But what makes those clean-cut West European bomber pilots creating their firestorms on the ground in which hundreds died, so much less primitive than the Balkan fanatics who burnt each others houses with people still inside, in a manipulated frenzy. I have in my career met both types and there is of course no way that these civilised well-shaved young pilots could have acted with the anger and passion of the dirty unshaven young men of the Balkans in setting fire to their neighbour's houses. But so what? Western culture gives rise to men who would never have the anger and passion to burn people alive – but when it comes to taking remote steps to burn those same people alive by pressing buttons then neither they, nor their wives, nor their sisters feel too bad about it.

Certainly my reflections have taken me back to the NATO bombing offensive against what was left of Yugoslavia – by then simply a truncated Serbia. I remain appalled by the decisions made, and even at the time, just before Harriet's massive second stroke, I was equally appalled. I could see how skilfully NATO's political leadership was manipulating the British media. Look let me be clear. I knew from my observations and all my contacts how fatal the power-crazy Milosovic was to the cause of a multi-national Bosnia or Kosovo. Nevertheless, when he and his government rejected the arrangements proposed at the Rambouillet conference –the issue which triggered the start of the bombing campaign – consider what they were being asked to accept. This was Chapter 7, Appendix B of the protocol, and I am quoting it absolutely verbatim –

"Nato forces will occupy Kosovo and will be immune from all legal process of any kind - civil or criminal. They will have the unimpeded right to move their vehicles and their equipment throughout the whole of the federal Republic of Yugoslavia. Nato is hereby granted the unrestricted use of all airports, roads, railways and ports without having to pay any fees or charges to the government of Yugoslavia or to any individual."

An Italian General, who had been involved earlier with a UN mission, commented that the Yugoslav government had after all by then agreed to abide by almost all the terms demanded by the Nato leaders at the Conference. But in the end they could not agree to the stationing of Nato forces on their sovereign soil on the terms proposed in Appendix B. There is really no doubt that no responsible government anywhere in the world could have accepted what was being proposed. What immediately followed the rejection by Yugoslavia was Nato's massive bombing offensive – a reaction which appeared to me – and still does – no different from the morality of the original actions of Serb forces.

But what then about all those terrible stories about atrocities committed on the ground by those dirty uncivilised Balkan peasants. In this case Serbs. I remember it all so well – the mass graves which were going to be uncovered, the bodies tossed into vats of sulphuric acid in the Tripca mines, the masses of corpses and what the urbane Nato spokesman Jamie Shea, said was 100,000 Kosovo Albanians unaccounted for. At least our civilised bombing campaign was going to put an end to all that and deal with the perpetrators. But what actually happened once the investigators got to look at the facts. First the 100,000 slaughtered became 10,000. Then it appeared that that too was just part of the manipulation. That figure was eventually whittled down to 1,800 bodies, furthermore it was completely unclear whether they were Serbs or Albanians. No mass graves – not a single one. No bodies in the Tripca mines. No vats of sulphuric acid. But of course by then the concerned compassionate Western public, led by their media, had found something else for their tender consciences to fasten on. So none of the actual facts as they came out got any publicity.

I thought that as I grew older and had to think more and more about my body and its aches and pains that I would become cooler, wiser and more mature in some way. But somehow this has not happened. In fact I seem to get more angry at what I consider to be injustice or something morally unacceptable. I can't pinpoint the moment that this has crept up on me – all I know is that I don't seem to have achieved that "serene which men call old age", as Rupert Brooke put it.

A week after the signing of the peace that ended the bombing campaign, it became clear that I would not have another assignment, and that I would have to retire. I decided that it was now the moment when I should make an effort and visit the Republic of Armenia, which had after all now been an independent country for several years. It was a decision that had much to do with what I had learnt about myself during that drastic week in Istanbul. It was not that I had consciously avoided going to Armenia before then – it was just that the occasion had not arisen, nor had I had the time available for a three week exploration.. Harriet had had her first stroke and could not travel, but she was doing fairly well and my absence would not be too difficult.

I was interested in what would be my own reaction. After considering all my feelings and suppressed anger about the children of the mixed marriages in the former Yugoslavia – what about me! It now appeared that I was myself a result of a loving union between two of perhaps the deepest ethnic hatreds of the early twentieth century – that between Armenians and Turks. Was my passion about the tragic situation for children of Serbo-Croat families perhaps a reflection of what was my own position. Was this discovery about my genes what had always made me so obsessed about 'identity'. I decided that I might find out by going to the Caucasus to see if I recognised any roots.

Chapter 16

Rasimir's taped statement to the Police

What do you mean – who am I? I am who I am – dark hair, fair skin, feverish eyes or so I'm told. My name is Rasimir sometimes referred to by my parents and some friends for some reason as Rasmi. I am 17 years old – soon to be 18. Oh – I see – you want to know to which community I belong. My father was a Croat and my mother was a Serb. I was living with my parents in Zagreb in 1992 when Croatia finally broke away from the federal republic of Yugoslavia – but look we were fooled. What Tudjman gave us – well why shouldn't I say 'us' – I am after all as much Croat as Serb – was not democracy. My Dad too always said that we became less free under Tudjman than we were under Tito. My Dad said that under Tito and his immediate successors, academics, journalists and poets could write about and discuss everything in public. But that under Tudjman everyone became intimidated not so much by direct official censorship so much as by officially inspired public nationalist intimidation, which Dad always said is much worse. It became impossible to criticise the new independent Croatia – even constructive criticism intended to improve aspects of the new state.

I have to accept that my poor father was obviously prejudiced, as after teaching history at the University for over twenty years, he was summarily dismissed under the Tudjman regime. He always complained that this was because he refused to fill his student's minds with the nationalistic myths of the past. He refused to spend his time forever teaching his classes of the nasty things that the 'Chetniks' had done to their grandparents.

Yes well of course I know that they are not all just myths. No look - I may be young but I am not confused. What the people in Brussels and the Western capitals wanted the world to think was that Croatia had been liberated from Communist oppression. But it was not true. Tito's leadership worked as beneficently as possible in what amounted to a dictatorship for the benefit of everyone. OK - it was an economic shambles but he did give everyone a genuine shared identity.

What do you mean – an illusion. Isn't all society a sort of shared illusion?

What happened to us as a family in Zagreb was that in the midst of all the nationalistic euphoria we had to pretend not to be of a mixed background. It was very stressful and even at the age of ten I felt a sort of shame because of my half-Serb make-up.. I knew and visited my Croat grandparents in the countryside – but I also occasionally went and stayed for a week or two with my Serb grandparents who lived in Bosnia. Suddenly there were citizens of Zagreb, I among them, who found that because their father and mother had come from say Belgrade sometimes even as long as forty years before, they were no longer welcome, and indeed were specifically made to feel unwanted. "What percentage of Serb are you?" was a phrase that I heard more than once. I should add that my Croat grandparents never once uttered a disparaging remark against me or my Mum, and even at my age I could see that they despised Tudjman and his petty bourgeois prejudices. But that didn't apply to most people in Zagreb

In the end my parents felt that they had to leave. My father said that going to Belgrade was going to be no better. There, the devious and manipulating Milosevic was exploiting the nationalist myth, every bit as fanatically as Tudjman, with the sole purpose of staying in power. So Dad decided to take us to Sarajevo in Bosnia – then still part of Yugoslavia. He managed to get a job at the University there – though he had to accept a demotion to the post of junior lecturer. Me? Well of course I didn't like it much. At nine or ten years old you have rather intense friendships with other boys of your own age, and I hated leaving them, when we left Zagreb. Of course they were all Croat boys – but so what, they were good friends.

Yes I know we were in no way unique – many mixed marriages were split by the conflicts that broke out after 1991 and continued during the rest of the nineties. Families were separated, sometimes enforced, sometimes by mutual consent. Relationships couldn't take the strain that was being imposed on them by their leaders and by the excitable media. Furthermore, you know, we didn't live in a vacuum – we were aware of what the world media was reporting, we had access to the internet and we were particularly aware of what the Western press was saying. The point I am making is that we were not only being manipulated by our own leaders, but we were regularly being fed on the continual stress of the West European media – press and TV – going on and on about how we all really hated each other. For ordinary people like me and my family it was simply not true. Certainly my parents did eventually separate under the strain when I was 12, but I know, God I know, I know that in those days in Zagreb before the break-up and the glorious independent nation-state that Tudjman achieved, they loved each other.

What do you mean – misplaced idealistic vision of your parents. Like all children I would have known, I would have been well aware if they had quarrelled. No, the strain of those bloody Bosnian Serbs bombarding the town from the hills above, and everything else happening around them, proved too much for their relationship, and my mother left us. Yes of course I am half Serb – but so what, their particular brand of nationalistic fervour is no better than that of the Croats. There they were those Serbs, being forced to become more and more nationalistic and xenophobic; urged to contemplate their great historic importance as defenders of European culture and Christianity against the unspeakable Turk. What utter bullshit!

Yes I went to school when we were living in Sarajevo. I made as many friends with other boys of my age as I had in Zagreb. They were Muslims. We called them Turks. All right, all right I had no idea then that it was not politically correct to refer to them that way. Bosniaks then – though we never used that term. You are one aren't you? I had many Muslim friends at school.

When I was nearly 12 I went to stay for a week with a boy who was at the same school and who lived with his grandparents during the term time, but who went home to his parents during the school holidays. They lived in Mostar; East Mostar of course. Had the beautiful Ottoman bridge connecting the two parts of the town been demolished by the Croats then? I don't know, I can't remember. What I do remember is the day we made an excursion to a nearby village – Stolac. This would be about August 1993 – I was 12 years old I took in everything. Four exquisite Ottoman mosques in the town had been blown up by some Croatian soldiers. They had then gone through the town rounding up and terrorizing all the Muslim women and children that they could lay their hands on. I couldn't bear to think about it. I think it was then that the anger and the madness began to come over me. Bosnians of every religion, yes yes even the Catholics, not just the Moslems, were proud of those four beautiful Ottoman mosques.

But none of those arrogant Westerners, blithely dropping their bombs on all of us in order to teach us not to be naughty, were ever aware of this. All they knew about were the graceful Ottoman bridges – particularly the iconic one at Mostar. How I hate them. No, no, not the senseless manipulated Croat vandals – the smug Westerners.

Yes, yes I know perfectly well that my father was not killed by Westerners. He was shot by some bloody Serb fanatic – a sniper in the hills taking potshots at people walking through the market square in the middle of the town. I was walking with him, through Markale the main outdoor market. It was very soon after my mother had left us. I suppose I was 11 or 12 – the chronology all gets a bit muddled in my mind. My Dad was holding my hand as we walked through the square picking our way through the mounds of fruit and vegetables. Suddenly there was a lot of shooting. By then I knew well the difference between local gunfights and the shots from snipers up in the hills. This was sniper fire. My Dad reacted quickly, turning to protect me by falling over me to bring us both down to the ground. But he got a bullet in the back as we both fell. He died instantly, at least I think so as he never said another word. The shooting eventually stopped. I crawled out from underneath him and sat by his side in a state of terror in the middle of that open space – but now I was holding his hand rather than the other way round. I don't know how long I sat there – how do you expect me to remember that. Eventually some Red Cross workers came round, prised my hand away from my dad's and they took my father away.

After that I began living for a short time with those same Muslim grandparents of my close schoolfriend whose parents lived in Mostar. But soon my mother got to hear about what had happened and managed to arrange to come and pick me up. I suppose I was 13 or 14 when I went to live with her in Belgrade. My experiences were driving me frantic. I no longer had any friends and I was burning with enormous resentments all the time. Of course I went to school again – now a Serb school in Belgrade. I also began reading avidly. Over a whole century the so-called Great Powers, what we all refer to nowadays as the international community – bloody smug westerners would be another name - have intervened massively in the region known as the Balkans where I and my family lived. They have deployed their own violence or excited violence between us, and have then retreated from the consequences of their original intervention.

Three times already before these latest interventions! Look I'm not an uneducated slob. I've read my history and it's all been explained to me by my teachers. Of course I respect my teachers, why shouldn't I?

First at the Congress of Berlin when entirely in their own interests they agreed to replace the waning Ottoman power with a series of competing little nation-states, each one connected to one or other of the Powers.

Then the Great War and Versailles – the Peace to end all peace – ending up with Lausanne and population exchange.

Then came the third of those previous interventions, which started with Italy's invasion of Greece and ended with a German takeover of most of the area. Each of these Great Power interventions into the land in which I live have been so destructive that they have left the area backward. The violence involved has ensured the continuation of deep civil and nationalistic conflicts. See here – I know I became bitter, I know that I am in deep trouble, but I do know that no Westerner – German,

British, French, or American for a single moment sees our troubles as due to all their own external interventions – now surpassed by this latest bombing campaign. On the contrary they continually go on about us all being motivated by a sort of genetic bloodthirstiness. We are all culprits with only ourselves to blame, who somehow force all those kindly and concerned outside Powers into having to intervene.

I know nothing about Albanians. I know nothing about Kosovo. All I know is that I sat underneath the rubble of our modest house in the outskirts of Belgrade after the Nato bombs had demolished it. Mistake! – rubbish – in any case so what. My mother had been in the same room but somehow the explosion and the falling concrete blocks had got her and had just missed me, though I was pinned under all the fallen rubble unable to move. My father had died instantly in Sarajevo, but my poor frail mother – bloodthirsty intransigent Balkan peasant according to Western propaganda – died in terrible pain and agony as her stomach spilled slowly out. What could I do? I couldn't even reach out to touch her hands. I lay there and listened for over an hour to my mother's screams, turning eventually to moans as her little strength began to give way.

I was 16. I was already mad with the injustice of what had been going on around me and of the way that my life had collapsed. This was the reality behind all that so-called humanitarian motivated intervention. God how I hated them – those smug Western readers of newspapers, becoming outraged and wanting their governments 'to do something about it'. I never recovered from those two days that I spent in that rubble, watching my mother die in agony and then lying with her corpse alongside me as I waited for rescue.

I know that none of this is any excuse for what I have

done. I don't deny the deliberate killing, nor do I deny the innocence of the young man I killed – but then so was my mother equally innocent. I have to add that at least I have achieved a sort of inner peace. I don't care anymore. I don't care. Somehow the nightmares at least have passed.

Chapter 17

Conrad's Search – the start

Identity? Every one of us has a unique identity – it's the basic human condition. But inevitably there are aspects of our identity which we share with others. Even in simple physical matters – like I clearly belong to the same group that is male, has black hair, dark eyes and a wide mouth. I share these easy identifying features with perhaps millions. But that's too simple – what about character – what about that favourite of the nation-state enthusiasts – nationality and race. What is it that is so important that makes a person living in Palestine a Jew or an Arab, or a resident of Sarajevo a Serb or a Croat or something different again. Why is 'race' or 'nationality' felt to be so important an aspect of ones identity.

Is it a matter of genetic inheritance? For the answer to that I go back to the question posed by the baby born of deceased English missionaries in war-torn China and brought up from the age of one by caring Chinese parents. The little boy will clearly have European features as he grows up – but will his genes make any difference as to how his character develops. Unlikely! What we get from our parents, and also our grandparents cousins and other members of our extended family is cultural. Then when we go to school and enter public life it becomes a matter of what we are taught and what we imbibe from our peers. So whether your parents are Serb or Croat, it is how you are educated, how you are nurtured and how you view your peer group that matters. But does that mean that genetic make-up plays no part in the development of your identity, and only affects your physical make-up.

I find myself puzzling over these issues more and more as I ponder on the fact that it now turns out that I have no English in my own genes at all. Stavros, it seems, was talking rubbish when he continually teased me about what he would refer to as my 'cold English blood'.

Quite why this decided me to explore the one side of my genetic make-up which had always been clear and remained so despite the lady Yasmin's revelations – namely my Armenian side inherited from my Avakian mother. Perhaps, I thought, if I went to visit the new Republic in the Caucasus I might also come to understand and have some empathy for the whole issue of the 'nation-state' with which I have had so little sympathy in my life so far. Perhaps there is something magical in the land itself which might in some mystical way help me to define and modify my sense of identity.

It is all so complex. Even though it turns out that I have not a drop of English genes in me, have I not thrilled in my youth at John of Gaunt's speech to Richard ll -

"...this sceptered isle, this earth of majesty, this seat of Mars, this other Eden, demi-paradise......this blessed plot, this earth, this realm, this England."

My noisy ebullient younger brother Billy, who after all was indeed genuinely half English, used to laugh at me if I ever quoted these lines. But I loved them –and if after I left the army my enthusiasm might have tempered a bit, as a teenager I was utterly elated like so many others.

So is it just the accident of where you happen to have been born and to have lived out your childhood, which is the principle factor in shaping your identity. Well I felt that I now had to find out. This is the sort of thing that is unimportant as you live your full life but which looms larger as you get older. So it was that soon after I returned from my last assignment in the former Yugoslavia and now at an age where I no longer stride out confidently, at an age when I have to get up and pee at least once, sometimes more, during the night, I set out to see if I recognised any of those 'roots' that so many people talk about. Harriet had had her first stroke, but was quite comfortable and encouraged me to go for the three weeks that I envisaged.

I arrived – as almost everyone does – into the airport at Yerevan at 2.00am. That first morning I followed my usual practice when arriving in a strange city of wandering out of my hotel and walking about blindly in order to get an immediate feel of a place. That first morning was a glorious day with a bright blue sky. My jaded London lungs were immediately struck by the brightness and sharpness of the air. Yerevan, although a city on a fairly flat plain, is already about 4,000 feet above sea-level and has a sharp dry climate. From the start I had this feeling of a complete sense of security – a feeling fairly rare when exploring newly visited cities. This sense of safety, so far as the surrounding population was concerned was not because they were particularly friendly and smiling or anything like that but because they appeared so calm and did not stare at me or impinge on my privacy in any way.

The streets were full of smart women all well and fashionably dressed in smart casual western-style clothes. I found many of them to be stunningly beautiful, even if a bit heavily made-up with strong lipstick, but having a provocative confidence as they walked the streets on their way to work or whatever. On the other hand the men in the streets did not seem to share that smartness and confidence. They wore dark and rather conservative clothes. A surprisingly large number of them had ties and somewhat shabby dark suits. Furthermore a significant number had not shaved. This was not a matter of 'designer stubble' – it just added to the rather shabby look of many of them. My mind went to the rather similar way in which men in the Balkans also often did not shave in the morning. I had come to the conclusion then that in countries where men had very dark hair, they would often need to shave again if they were going out in the evening and so didn't bother to shave in the mornings.

All this gave an immediate gender contrast on the Yerevan streets which was quite startling. In addition to the difference in the style and confidence of those who were on the streets there was a clear inbalance of the sexes. It was not only that there were more girls and women than men, but there was also a clear shortage of young men and this accentuated the contrast. The fall of the Soviet empire was only ten years ago and there were two factors still working to accentuate the shortage of young men – first the war with Azerbaijan meant that many young men were in the army, and then, secondly, once they came out of the army there was no work in the country and so many of them worked abroad, sending remittances home. The men in the streets were clearly bruised by their inability to provide for their families, and had the sad eyes of the perennially unemployed.

The current independent Republic of Armenia, the final resting place of the nation was until eighty or so years ago very much the fringe area of the Armenian people. Wealthy merchants from Constantinople, or the sophisticated middle class of Van or Erzurum looked upon the Yerevan Oblast of the Russian Empire as the distinctly poor country cousins of the Armenian nation. It was, however, the geographic area which contained within it the centre of the Armenian Apostolic Church, together also with the iconic symbol of Mount Ararat.

The cream of the Armenian people – the doctors, the great trading houses, the lawyers, the architects and so on were those who were part of and lived within the Ottoman Empire. Yerevan was a tiny backwater throughout the nineteenth century and could in no way compare with the great Armenian cities like Van or Kars, or with the old and long-established Armenian population in Constantinople.

During the heyday of the Ottomans, the Armenians together with the Greeks constituted the middle class of the Empire. They provided the bankers, the merchants, the architects and the traders, otherwise lacking in Ottoman society where there was always a yawning gap between the Beys and Pashas of Stamboul on the one hand and the Turkish peasantry of Anatolia on the other.

The Armenian plateau in Eastern Anatolia was peopled by a very mixed population of Armenians, Turks and Kurds. Until towards the end of the nineteenth century they lived, if not amicably, at least fairly tolerantly together. This was all changed by the advent of a new Sultan – Abdul Hamid II – who created a huge spy network to reinforce his despotic rule and who deliberately fostered race hatred between his peoples – rather, dare I say it, like Tudjman and Milosevic – as a means of reinforcing his own power. The persecutions of the 1890's gave rise, as a reaction, to the start of a nineteenth century nationalism amongst a population originally quite ready to live as part of a multi-national empire.

In 1908, following a revolt in the Turkish garrison in Salonika, a revolution broke out which became known as the 'Young Turk' movement. The odious Abdul Hamid was eventually forced to abdicate and a constitution was declared. It appeared that a new liberal dawn had burst out in the old Empire. The Armenians, Greeks and Jews of Constantinople welcomed this revolution and there was dancing in the streets – but it was an illusion. As had happened before in Europe during the nineteenth century, a popular liberal movement turned into a 'people's' nationalism often worse than the absolutism it replaced. So, the bumbling and inefficient, but largely tolerant multi-national Ottoman Empire, was replaced by the fascistic and fanatic Ittihad government, espousing in due course a particularly virulent Turkic nationalism. This all resulted in the terrible events of 1915 which settled the Armenian question in Anatolia once and for all with the twentieth century's first murderous brutal ethnic cleansing. The entire Armenian population of Eastern Anatolia numbering over two million disappeared – most of them brutally disposed of in death marches into the Syrian desert. Some, however, fled and escaped into Russia where they swelled the numbers and forever changed the character of the old Tsarist Oblast of Yerevan.

Like in Sicily I found that Armenia appeared to have jumped from a poor quality telephone landline stage straight into the mobile phone era. Everyone has a mobile phone. However, unlike Sicily, they use them in a most discreet fashion, instead of walking down the street making a grand operatic show of talking animatedly on the phone waving their arms around as they do in Italy. This was also part of the feeling of calm and relaxation, which made such an impressive first impression. I have never before been in a largish city (Yerevan has more than a million people) where the noise of the birds roosting in the many trees dotted about the streets was so clear and penetrating. The streets were full of trees in full bloom and there were a great number of small outdoor cafes, each having four or five tables under large red coca-cola umbrellas – never more than a few yards from the next one. They serve traditional Ottoman Turkish coffee – but don't ask for Turkish coffee, ask for Armenian coffee.

In my wanderings I eventually found myself at the bottom of a monstrous concrete flight of steps going up a hillside, built to commemorate some Soviet anniversary. Originally intended as a huge fountain with water cascading down, it has in fact only worked as a fountain once. The present government could clearly never afford to run it as such ever again. It was crumbling away and was immensely ugly. Ugly or not I simply had to climb it, as the view from the top where there appeared to be some sort of monument was likely to be impressive. As I climbed those concrete steps Mount Ararat, which I had forgotten about till then, began to appear behind me in the distance over the roofs of the city. In the heat of midday as i climbed, the view of that snow-capped peak, shimmering and seeming to float in the sky was truly magnificent. It is rare to make out the slopes leading up to the peak in the summer due to the heat haze, and so the stunning top of the mountain seems to float in the air above the town. Ararat is with you all the time whenever you are in the Yerevan plain.

Chapter 18

Conrad searching

The next day I took a walk down to the River Hrazdan. This river runs through an attractive gorge which goes through and alongside the town. As this was still early summer the water was running fast and noisily alongside banks of grass filled with poppies and wild flowers. Anywhere else this would be a real feature but here it has become a neglected corner – though this could of course change in the future.

Wherever you come across the crumbling ruins of almost any major past imperial state – Persian – Ottoman – Mughal - even British-Indian, the remnants of the disappeared empire often become a major attraction and are rarely ugly. What exists here in Armenia, however, are the crumbling ruins of the Soviet Communist Empire, and they are at their worst alongside the lovely Hrazdan river. Both here and all over Armenia there are great fallen concrete slabs – rusting pipes – collapsing and ugly public buildings now fulfilling no purpose and originally built without any regard for any environmental consideration; empty and decrepit factories rotting away all over the place. So here, almost in the middle of the city, runs this attractive gorge with wonderful overgrown bushes, trees and banks of poppies. But instead of a beautiful old wall, or a graceful arched bridge, or a leafy tended path, one picks one's way up and over crumbling concrete pipes and collapsing structures, built originally for heaven knows what purpose, but no longer of any use to anyone at all.

Once over the worst of the industrial ruins, walking along a recognisable path I met and chatted with several elderly men who were clearly taking a favourite daily walk, picking the wild flowers and stopping and staring at the rushing river below them. On the other side of the river there was a party of young boys who were daring each other to pass a rather alarming but tethered guard dog, looking for a way to get through to the bank from where they could have a dip in the river. But once again there was this contrast between the boys on the one hand and the rather shabby unemployed elderly men on the other – there seemed to be nothing in between.

It turns out that a very high proportion of the young men are away in the army- and that in addition, due to the lack of employment, a large number are working abroad. These are not families who have emigrated to the fleshpots of California, these are single men who have gone, not to settle down but to work, mainly in Russia and the Ukraine, where their high-tech skills and literacy are in good demand. These young men regularly send money back to their families and it is this regular infusion of income into the extended family which allows the girls and women, who are employed in secretarial, teaching and nursing jobs, to be so smart and confident.

I stopped and chatted with one or two of these elderly retired men. One in particular gave me a .lot of his time. Eighty years old and still healthy meant that he was born in 1919 or thereabouts. He told me that he had been born in Aleppo. His parents were survivors from one of the death marches leading to the Syrian desert. Those that made it to Aleppo were the lucky ones as opposed to the large number that died in Deir-ez-zor and in the desert. He himself did not know where his parents were from in Ottoman Turkey originally. Why? I wondered – had he never asked or had they simply clammed up like so many of the other survivors of ethnic cleansings of this sort. He himself had come to Soviet Armenia from Syria after the second world war. Despite having lived in Yerevan now for over fifty years, he still called himself a 'returnee'.

The path I was following, surrounded by industrial waste was now joined by an overgrown old railway line which must at one time have connected the main line to the now abandoned factories. It was a narrow gauge line which appeared to be totally abandoned. However to my surprise, as I walked along I noticed the same elderly gentlemen every so often bending down and pulling up weeds growing near or over the tracks and throwing them to one side. Suddenly there was a deep rumbling noise and round the corner ahead of me came a great diesel railway engine pulling along very slowly a couple of open flat trucks with railings round them, filled with a group of joyous six-year olds. They all waved at me with great grins as the train slowly trundled past going nowhere as I knew well. I walked on and eventually reached the derelict little station where this train had originated and which was now part of a Park for children – the train being simply a fun ride for kids. It now became clear why the old men were clearing the weeds as they walked along – doing something which the municipality could not afford to do, to help keeping the line just about functioning.

I walked out of the park and took a minibus back to my hotel. The transport system in the city is interesting. Yerevan's old and decrepit soviet-era buses and trams clearly could not cope with the demands of an increasingly mobile population looking for work anywhere within the city and needing to be able to move around to get there when they found a job. There was nothing the cash-strapped municipality could do about it except to keep the buses going even though they have long since passed their sell-by date. The entrepreneurial spirit of the locals has come into play. Little vans – people-movers in the west – with the back seats adapted to make it easier to get in and out and seating about eight crisscross the city in clearly accepted and numbered routes. There are over one hundred of these routes, and the route number with the name of the terminals at each end and three or four of the principal roads passed to get from one end to the other is clearly printed and attached to the side windows. These private mini-buses run very frequently and work on the old-fashioned system of supply and demand. The cost when I was there, however far or short you go was a fixed 100 dram – then about 12p. You can hail the bus anywhere like a taxi and you can get off anywhere along the route.

I found, even by my second day, that there was a calm, relaxed and unagressive atmosphere in the streets. This is repeated in these little buses. This was not an exuberantly latin or mediterranean population, nor a noisy and argumentative middle eastern one. The little buses are silent, the passengers reserved almost to the extent of being withdrawn and are very careful to recognise and not impinge on each other's space. Friendly and warm they may be when approached directly, particularly if you need help, nevertheless they are all reserved and respect each other's privacy.

Next to the covered market there is the highly-coloured façade of an old Persian Mosque. This was built in 1765 by the then Persian Governor of Yerevan whilst it was part of the Persian Empire. When the Russian empire absorbed Yerevan in the 1820's it began to be used as a Russian Orthodox church. With the coming of the revolution and the introduction of communism, it was abandoned and fell into decay. In due course

Stalin ordered it to be pulled down. I am thrilled and strangely comforted by discovering that the citizens of Yerevan, whilst not daring openly to oppose Stalin's order directly, nevertheless put sufficient obstacles in the way year after year so that the old mosque never actually got pulled down. In the same way, and with similar courage, the Christian citizens of Cordoba rose up and threw out of their town the workers and soldiers sent by the King and the Inquisition in Madrid to pull down their beautiful mosque, which is accordingly still standing. Similarly the original minaret and the dome of the mosque in Yerevan remained despite Stalin's order, though the lovely garden and surrounding arches were in ruins. The Iranian government offered to fund the complete restoration of the building and gardens – known as the Blue Mosque - and already the coloured tiles are back and the gardens have reverted to a beautiful and peaceful haven.

So, here in the middle of this obsessively Christian nation is a beautiful example of the basic tolerance of ordinary people, unwilling to buckle under to the demand for uniformity within the nation-state. People recognise and respond to beauty, even if that beauty arises out of the culture of people whom ranting nationalist leaders and fanatical clerics are telling them are their natural enemies.

Chapter 19

Conrad's search – The problem of Aid

The remittances of all those young men working in Russia and the former Soviet Republics is not the only hard currency that rolls into the republic. There is also a large Armenian diaspora numbering well over a million dotted around the world. These are largely old Ottoman Armenians whose family never had any contact with the Yerevan oblast prior to their forced departure from the lands they originally inhabited. They contribute millions of dollars by way of charitable donations to the Armenian state, funding such things as roads, bridges, schools and hospitals. I decided on my third day to join a western-organised group, who had come to Armenia to inspect and be shown round various projects which their local communities in the West had been funding. I clambered into the bus and met one representative from California, two from the American East Coast, a lady representing the Argentinians, two gentlemen from Switzerland, a Dutchman and an English Solicitor and a somewhat strident lady teacher from Manchester, amongst others all from the West.

Armenian was the only common language, but some people could either not speak Armenian at all, or like me had only a fairly limited knowledge. At one time I overheard the lady representing the large and powerful Argentinian lobby talking French with the German delegate who could not himself speak English. It reminded me of Bolis fifty years ago, where people automatically switched from one language to another without conscious thought, in order to accommodate new arrivals who spoke a different language

151

Our first visit was to the children's hospital in Yerevan, the refurbishing of which was one of the special projects being funded by the Argentinians. We were welcomed, like at all such functions in Armenia, with great formality and handshakes all round. We then moved in. The atmosphere of goodwill and jollity amongst our group vanished. The contrast between the newly-built Argentinian sections and the old broken down and truly miserable Soviet wards was enormous.

At first one would have thought that this might have appeared as a source of self-congratulation for all these collective western fund-raisers – but another factor intervened. The Argentinians had plumped for a scheme whereby they funded the rebuilding of the hospital, section by section, floor by floor, instead of gutting and doing up the whole at one fell swoop. The rationale was obvious and reasonable, as in that way the hospital could continue to function as each section was renewed. So what we were seeing was a hospital divided into three different areas – the new and completed sections – the old and as yet untouched ex-soviet sections - and the one section where work was currently being carried out for the refurbishment.

In one of the newly completed sections, supposedly fully functioning, we saw ten rooms with two beds in each – state-of-the-art children's wards with beds for mothers – two spotless tiled bathrooms and a whole lot of other hospital rooms all within the one floor. I counted eight nurses or cleaners, I couldn't tell the difference as they all wore similar white coats. There appeared also to be four Doctors present, though I suspect one or two of them might have come from other areas to look at us, as we were looking at them.

This floor had been completed fifteen months before, but there was only one patient in the whole section

– a little boy in bed, with his mother sitting beside him chatting.

Yet the beds in the old ugly and shabby soviet-style wards were all filled with children of all ages. As a group we could not understand why, and despite urging the Argentinian representative to make enquiries I am still not sure that I fully understood it then. The Director of the hospital who was hovering as we were taken round was either unable or unwilling to make any cogent reply to our questions.

I worked it out later. It would appear that at this stage in the life of the new State the government simply could not afford any sort of free health service for anybody beyond the age of five and accordingly everyone else has to pay. But the result was that on the face of it the Argentinians had been working to fund the construction of something which at the end would only be used by the well-off. The hospital was clearly charging patients for the new refurbished wards considerably more than they were charging for the old and decrepit soviet ones.

Time and again I came across this dilemma. It is one thing to build a new hospital – quite another to staff it and maintain it at a high standard. Later on this first day we went on to a small section of the University building. This was intended as a special library and study-room for a particular subject which I no longer recall. It was being funded by New York Armenians. This worked well as, once finished, it was a complete and functioning unit requiring the minimum of maintenance. We also saw some new road and bridge repairs being paid for by general funds raised by the western diaspora, which seemed to me to be more useful than state-of-the-art hospital wards. Transport is a vital part of any country's infrastructure to enable the hospitals and schools to function in the first place. Yet, if in London or Buenos

Aires or New York you try to persuade people to make a donation, they will fork out happily for a children's hospital or for a new school, but will not be so generous for another fifty miles of good firm roads. There are ten hospitals in Yerevan, all in a varying state and condition – and there are many doctors. However for a hospital to function properly, someone has to pay the staff, maintain the new equipment and employ doctors. It is the cost of all this that is lacking – for the moment – not the building and equipment itself.

I would not want to exaggerate the problem. It seemed to apply particularly to the medical field. The new schools being built with Aid money are well-filled and adequately staffed with teachers who are obviously being paid by someone. The difference seems to lie in the fact that at the moment health cannot be free, whilst education at least up to 12 has to be. I have little doubt that it will all work out in the end.

This same evening I went to a concert at the Yerevan concert Hall. The Armenian Philharmonic Orchestra was performing Beethoven's 3rd and Tchaikovsky's 6th symphonies. It was billed to be the last major concert before an enormous refurbishment, projected and being paid for by an American millionaire, which was going to take over a year to complete during which time the Concert Hall and the Opera House which are back to back and part of the same fairly impressive structure built in the 1920's, would be closed. The two buildings have had scarcely any maintenance almost since they were first built seventy years ago at the start of the Soviet period. The seats were threadbare and all the numbers have fallen off, save for one or two dotted here and there. Accordingly when looking for your seat you count from the few that are still there.

However in fairness this was one of the few success

stories of the Soviet period. The Communist system un-questionably removed the elitist element in audiences for concerts, ballet and opera. The most expensive seats for the concert I went to were 2,000 dram – then less than £3, and you could get in for as little as 400 dram, then about 45p. I know that these prices consti-tute much more for the locals than they do for visitors. Nevertheless, by any possible standards of comparison it was still remarkably cheap. There was a good attend-ance both at this concert and for the ballet that I had gone to the night before. It was clear that all sections of society were attending.

On the next day we drove off into the countryside, heading for the northern provinces which was the area that had been devastated by the great earthquake of twelve years before. The Armenian countryside to the northwest is almost totally treeless, although in spring all the hills were covered in a light coating of grass and wild flowers. Stony and criss-crossed with ravines I had the impression that it went on for miles right across to Anatolia and to Lake Van. The landscape was empty save for large herds of sheep managed by one solitary shepherd and possibly his son. This was open nomadic land and had been for centuries. But increasingly farm-ers have ploughed strips along the river valleys and marked out fields. More and more land is coming into private ownership and since the fall of the soviet system the food production of Armenia has tripled in only ten years.

From the very start of the journey, immediately af-ter leaving the outskirts of Yerevan, the first impression that strikes the visitor is the terrible environmental dis-aster of the Soviet industrial system. Block after block of abandoned derelict concrete factories are dotted almost at random over what would otherwise be a wild and attractive countryside. Lines of ugly electricity pylons march across the land without any regard to any environmental considerations – often pointlessly duplicated by other separate lines and now all useless and abandoned. The detritus of an abandoned industrial imperial society is truly awful. Sooner or later it will certainly be cleared, but for the moment it just has to stay rotting away as it cannot be a priority for such a poor country to mount any clearance program. Had the countryside been one with plenty of trees and bushes, the waste might have become more hidden and acceptable by the effect of overgrowing nature – but here the landscape whilst interesting in its shapes and contours is treeless and all those fallen blocks of reinforced concrete and rusted steel stand out without any hope at the moment of being softened by nature.

The hilly plain stretches for miles and is covered with stones, large and small. In order to cultivate anything they have to be removed. The soil, though fertile is so thin that this has to be done by hand, stone by stone, back-breaking work. Any heavy machines would tear up the soil as well as removing the stones. These stones reappear – they sort of rise up out of the soil – if the land is not continually cultivated by a devoted peasantry. The removal during the terrible events of 1915 of the basic Armenian peasantry from the Armenian heartlands of the Ottoman Empire has resulted in large areas of that part of the Armenian plateau still within Turkey being re-covered with all those stones, as the abandoned farms lie unworked and empty.

This part of Armenia is a land of wide views and is very different to other areas. Sweeping empty hills covered with snow in winter and with short vividly green mossy grass and wild flowers in summer. There are few humans around and accordingly one is even more aware of those that do appear, working in their cultivated strips and fields. I was told that I would note an inbalance of women to men working in the fields. However this was not my experience at all. It seemed to me as we passed that there was almost an equal number of men and women working together in the fields, and often one could see that it was a family group – certainly nothing like the gender inbalance in the streets of the towns. The only gender difference I did note was that the men were all using tools of one sort or another, whilst all the bending work using hands directly on the earth seemed to be being carried out by women. When I pointed this out, a buxom, lady sitting behind me called out very firmly and rather scornfully –

"Men can't bend you know."

Chapter 20

Conrad – Gyumri and Spitak

The earthquake that took place in 1987, 12 years before my visit, devastated a large area of Northern Armenia. It caused over 20,000 deaths and shattered the infrastructure and way of life of the whole region. The group I had joined were off to visit this area to inspect and open some of the projects being funded by the diaspora and some of its specific local committees.

We arrived in Spitak, a town which had been completely devastated and left in a total ruin. This small town was being rebuilt house by house. As a result of it having been totally razed to the ground, the town authorities were able to do some imaginative re-planning of the centre and of the streets. As we drove over the truly awful pot-holed road and down into the valley we were met by the local police chief, who then escorted our bus into town, horn blaring. In the new town centre stood an attractive building that was due to be ceremonially opened that very day.

Staring at us as we emerged from the bus was a group of about one hundred rather dumb-founded citizens – as always the men shabby and unshaven and the women smarter, though not in any way as chic as in Yerevan. After the usual ritual offering of a newly baked loaf and salt we all then moved into a beautifully constructed marble floored building. This was the new Cultural Centre which had been paid for by a very likeable modest Belgian gentleman, who was in our party with his two young sons and who gave a short speech in English after being welcomed by the Mayor. Speaking in English, as ironically he knew no Armenian and the mayor and the more educated citizens watching, knew no French but had a smattering of English. A young girl was playing Beethoven on a well-tuned grand piano as we all trooped in. We were followed in by over a hundred or so somewhat bemused citizens of the town.

I found myself contrasting the chandeliers and marble columns of this new Cultural Centre with the continued scenes of devastation outside. The old metal cabins put up immediately after the earthquake were still there after twelve years, and the number of new houses and apartment blocks completed was still fairly small. I overheard some rather vociferous elderly women muttering about the 'waste of money'. My first reaction at the time was to agree with them. It seemed incongruous to have built such a gorgeous building in a town where some of the most basic living accommodation was still in such short supply. However the new centre was going to include a disco, space for a video cinema, as well as a performance hall and music rooms. Most of the group disagreed with me and believed that it was a vital construct for the purposes of morale, particularly for the young who otherwise had nothing to do or nowhere to go in the evenings.

Driving out of Spitak, we passed the usual ex-soviet industrial wasteland. However, somehow, as all these old concrete blocks, rusting metal beams, and decrepit buildings had been totally ruined and collapsed right down to the ground by the earthquake, it was in a way less ugly than the still standing but derelict and abandoned factories of the rest of the country. We drove to our next destination, Gyumri, along a beautiful river valley. Wherever there was a flat area alongside the rushing river, plots of cultivated land, privately owned and farmed, were beginning to encroach on the ubiquitous stony pasture land.

Gyumri was one of the most visually depressing towns that I have ever visited. Spitak, by contrast, was not so depressing for a variety of reasons. Spitak was totally ruined and this means that the rebuilding going on dominates the town and not any old derelict buildings. Furthermore Spitak is much smaller and the countryside and the surrounding hills are always visible at the end of the streets, and this constantly tempers the views of the man-made mess and the ravages of nature's revenge. Gyumri however, was a large town and further away from the epicentre. The earthquake here was not quite so devastating. The shell of many of the buildings remain standing, but with all the floors inside collapsed and the walls cracked and leaning dangerously.

Had the government been strong and determined enough it might have been best if the ruined town had been totally abandoned and a completely new town built alongside. But that would have been an almost impossible solution. The people clung to their old and sometimes dangerous buildings till the last moment. Furthermore they could not be blamed for this reaction when the alternative was only tents and metal containers with windows in them, some of which were still in use twelve years after the earthquake, despite the fact that when they were originally provided by the international aid organisations, they had been given a maximum lifespan of only three years.

In the course of our drive through the old town, we passed a line of terraced houses built in black stone and with little gardens in front. This one line of neat houses was dominated by a huge collapsed factory right behind them and two high rise apartment buildings alongside, totally ruined and standing empty. Our driver pointed out these houses as being "tsarnikolain jamanag". He was referring to Tsar Nicholas' times. These old houses

– originally working class dwellings had stood up solidly to the quake, whilst all around them everything built in the soviet era was in ruins.

In a newly built area our cavalcade of seven cars now led by the Gyumri chief of police drove up to the "New Gyumri Arts College," yet another project financed by our modest Belgian friend. There was an enormous contrast of mood between the gloomy Westerners staring out at the crumbling town from their bus, and the local reception. The path up to the Centre was lined by young girls aged from eight to fourteen, waving balloons, calling out and laughing with the sheer joy of witnessing a spectacle. I have always been fairly cynical about these official jamborees where the great and the good posture and make banal speeches, while an audience look on indifferently, but these girls were smiling with pleasure and clearly enjoying themselves.

This was an Arts College and so they had a little band playing us in and there were even some boys in it trumpeting away. Inside everything was on display – paintings, sculpture, weaving, and above all music. There were about twenty practice rooms. Throughout my stay in Armenia I was totally overwhelmed by the love of music shown by everyone, poor and very poor alike. Every family tries to urge some musical instrument on each of their children, and clearly will make some sacrifices to acquire the necessary instrument and tuition.

The College gave us a little concert in the Performance area. When one stood there seeing all these girls enjoying themselves immensely, all immaculately turned out and then recalled the collapsed houses and the grey drab living conditions outside, it was very moving. The sheer exuberance of the human spirit and the stimulation it could get from simple cultural pursuits made me rethink my earlier reservations about the Spitak Cultural Centre. However, a cynic might add that it happened also to be the last day of term before the holidays.

As the concert came to an end the New York delegate, a young man with every stereotyped New York image you could hope for, slipped in beside me. I had noticed his absence from the bus in Spitak. He had overslept and missed the bus. Not to be defeated by such a banal event, he hired himself a car and a driver in order to catch us up and join us in Gyumri. Once there the elderly Armenian driver drove round the devastated town quite unable to find the new Arts College. He regularly stopped the car to ask directions from males in the streets, who true to the usual lack of young men were all elderly. Typically he did not accost any of the many young girls and women in the streets. He drove forlornly round and round as our New Yorker got more and more impatient. After ten to fifteen minutes of this our friend spotted yet another group of girls chatting on a street corner.

"Stop the fucking car," he shouted and jumped out. He harangued the girls in fairly good western Armenian, got clear if a bit giggly instructions repeated twice and proceeded to direct the somewhat embarrassed driver straight to our reception. Furthermore, to cap it, in relating this story to me he could not see why I found it so funny.

We all moved on back into the devastated old town centre where our last function of the day was to lay the foundation stone for a new kindergarten, paid for by the East Coast American committee. Here the ceremony took place in the middle of a total muddy dump surrounded by a miserable rusting metal construction which housed the current kindergarten. This was the really poor end of the town, but we still had all the welcoming speeches. There were great holes everywhere. The Belgian's two young sons clambered down into the deepest of these with a sealed pottery cask containing something or other but what I never found out. A large decrepit concrete-making machine which I had originally taken as a museum piece, then began turning and churning out concrete which almost fell on the boys before they managed to skip out having buried the cask.

Throughout all this I was left with one interesting question – where were the local boys?

We arrived back in Yerevan fairly late in the evening. Republic Square was closed to traffic so our bus could not get to the hotel and we had to walk. This was because a large end-of-term party was being held by Yerevan's student teenagers in the Square between 8.00pm and 11.00. Here at last, as I wandered out to watch, the gender balance was fairly equal. The last sleepy thought I had as I watched the exuberant dancing was – could you ever imagine the London police stopping all the traffic in say Trafalgar Square so that the city's teenagers and schoolchildren could have an end-of-term party. Never mind that – could anyone ever imagine the car and taxi drivers tolerantly laughing when having to spend the extra ten minutes to find another way round. I doubt if it is an attitude that will last as the town becomes more sophisticated.

Chapter 21

Razmik

I met Conrad effendi when he came with a party of British tourists to visit Sushi for a day during the summer of 1999. But I am not myself from Sushi. I was born in Sumgait in Azerbaijan and I was five years old when all the trouble arose there in 1988. My father was Armenian. I am not now exactly sure what race or nationality my mother was, though we all spoke Armenian at home. In those days prior to the fall of the Soviet Union it didn't matter like it does now. I know she came from Georgia, but I think she wasn't actually Georgian herself – Ossetian or something like that. I know people will say –

'What! you don't even know what community or culture your mother belonged to'

But I was only five, and at that age are you really concerned in any way as to what nationality your parents might be. The Soviet Union had not as yet imploded and we all lived in apartment blocks all mixed up together – Azeris mainly of course, but with many others – Armenians and Jews – jumbled in with Georgians and Russians.

I do know that it was winter when the troubles occurred as I remember being cold all the time. Until that time I had never felt any racial or national tension – certainly never anything directed against me. We boys in our apartment block would run and play together after school without any thought as to whether one was an Armenian or the other was an Azeri or a Jew. But looking back on it as Baron Conrad has asked me to do, I do now vaguely recall an increase in tension which pervaded the whole town, even though it did not affect our own games in and around the blocks. Of course I was not directly aware of it at the time but I know now how this was all being manipulated by Azeri leaders as a result of the growing conflict over the status of the Armenian enclave in Nagorno Karabagh. The rising tension was being created artificially for the sole purpose of giving them some extra clout in their negotiations with the soviet leaders in Moscow.

It started with demonstrations in Lenin Square. At first fairly mild they got more and more extreme as the crowds were deliberately inflamed by nationalist fervour. I remember on one occasion as I drifted down with two of my friends – both Azeris I think – and we listened on the outskirts of the crowd on the square. I heard the speaker ranting on about Armenians being better off and better educated than Azeris. I then heard shouts of –

"Death to Armenians!" "Armenians get out of our city"

Do you know somehow I didn't connect the shouts to me. Of course I knew I was Armenian – that my Dad was Armenian and that we spoke Armenian in the house and that I had just started at an Armenian school – but nevertheless, somehow I didn't think that the shouting was directed against me. What did it have to do with me; and so, completely oblivious, we played on.

Some years later I read an account written by an officer in the Soviet Ministry of Internal Affairs, which referred to the Sumgait demonstrations at the time in these terms –

"The atmosphere in these demonstrations was one of mass psychosis and hysteria in which the people felt they were required \to take revenge for their compatriots supposedly killed in Armenia and Nagorno-Karabakh. From the platform they would call for the duty of Muslims to come together in a war against the infidels. The passions were at their highest. The situation got out of control. All this allowed the organizers of these demonstrations to easily provoke a certain part of the Muslim population of the town to pogroms and murders of Armenians."

I cannot now remember the exact chronology of what happened on those terrible days, nor can I myself speak of anything beyond what I experienced with my own eyes. My parents and I were sitting in our apartment with the lights on. Sympathetic Azeri neighbours had warned my Mum not to go out and also not to turn our lights off. That night mobs - manipulated and deliberately enraged mobs - were rampaging through the streets seeking out ethnic Armenians with a view to beating them up. Being Armenian was the only criterion for being targetted – and the whole affair was supposed to be in revenge for Azeri deaths in Nagorno-Karabagh. I found out later that although Azeri deaths did undoubtedly take place, at this stage there had been none at all and this was all a government-inspired riot intended purely to strengthen their negotiating stance over the disputed region.

I will set out what happened to us, but to establish the background this is how it was reported in the Russian press -

"The anti-Armenian pogrom and violence started on the evening of February 27, one week after the appeal of the Council of People's Deputies to unite Nagorno-Karabakh with Armenia and according to many sources was a direct response to the Council's decision. The apartments of Armenians (which were marked in advance) were attacked and the residents were indiscriminately murdered, raped, and mutilated by the Azerbaijani rioters. Rodina (Motherland) magazine gave the following description of the events:

"In peacetime, the Soviet Union has never experienced what happened then. Gangs of about ten to fifty or more people raced through the city, broke windows, burned cars, but the main thing was that they were looking for Armenians. A number of sources testify that the pogrom was organized in advance instead of being a spontaneous action, the perpetrators had previously obtained the list of addresses of the Armenian residents of the city many of the perpetrators were armed with metal rods, axes, hammers and other such tools obtained from metal factories in advance, as well as rifles and guns. Most Armenians lived among their Azeri and Russian neighbors in apartments. The frenzied mobs would enter the apartment buildings where they would search to find out where Armenians lived. Often, the rioters would know in which apartments they lived, but those who took shelter amongst their Azeri and Russian neighbors, survived. Other attempts to exclude themselves from harm, which sometimes worked, included turning on the television to watch Azeri music concerts, raising the volume to give off the effect that Azeris resided in the apartment. Muslim women in the Caucasus had a long tradition of dropping their shawls and hair coverings on the ground as a gesture for men to abstain from participating in violence. Such efforts were made by some Azeri women in the corridors of the apartment blocks attacked but went largely unheeded by the men The rioters forced their way into the apartments and attacked the residents regardless.".

Well I myself can't say what happened anywhere else. I can only speak as to what I experienced. I was about to get my pyjamas to go to bed when my mother said –

"Razmik – don't get into your pyjamas for the moment – stay dressed but go and lie down and get some sleep."

I did so and I might have dozed off – I can't be sure – but I awoke to hear a loud banging on our door and a great crash. I jumped up and ran out to the sitting room which was immediately after the front door. The front door had been smashed in and there was a crowd of about twenty men who were pushing into the room. I suppose my Dad may have been standing in front of the door or trying to hold it back or something but he was lying on the floor with blood pouring from a knife still stuck in his chest. Even at only five years old I knew he was dead. My Mum was screaming and trying to get to Dad, but she was held back by a couple of the men.

Although only five years old I understood that my father had been killed by these men. However, I did not understand what they were doing to my Mum. I sat cowering in the corner. Why were they tearing off her clothes? I could hear our Azeri neighbours in the corridor – the women were screeching in their high ululating voices and, as I found out five minutes later, tearing off their shawls and throwing them on the floor. My mother was now almost naked. She had stopped screaming but was now crying. One of the men then said something indicating the women outside in the corridor. The other men nodded and then one of the men, helped by another, threw my Mum over his shoulder and they all clattered out causing all the women in the corridor to run off into their own flats.

What could I do. I was only five – not a helpless toddler admittedly, but still pretty raw. My Dad lay dead.

Our apartment was a complete shambles and even then I noticed that some of the men had gone off with things that belonged to my parents. What was I to do. My Mum's arms were trailing down the back of the bully who had draped her over his shoulder. I got up from where I had been squatting and ran straight out after them and followed them down the stairs and into the street where crowds were still roaming crying out slogans in which I heard the word for 'death' over and over again – but couldn't catch any of the other words.

It suddenly became vital for me to keep my mother in sight – but I was equally frightened that one of them might turn and see me. It was difficult as they were moving fast. But why? Why was my mother almost naked and where were they taking her. Ah of course the Hospital that was it. It is in hospitals that you have to take your clothes off.

But I was wrong – it all ended in a small local cemetery. There in a spot in the middle of the tombs they laid my mother on the ground and climbed on top of her one by one. I did not watch as I cowered on my knees behind a low stone wall. I could hear her moans and screams but I did not watch – I did not watch.

After they all trooped off whooping with more cries of 'death' death', I crept out from my wall and went and sat by my Mum. She was completely naked and covered in blood all over – all over. I took her hand and I believe she knew who it was. I had no idea what to do. I had no idea where to get help or how I could leave her anyway. I sat holding her hand for the rest of the night – and I know that she knew who it was, as early in the morning as the sun rose and shone on the apartment block opposite the cemetery I heard her whisper 'Razmik' and I am sure I felt a faint squeeze of my hand, before the end.

My mother was dead.

This was only the second day of the riots and there were still crowds of enraged men roaming the streets. I walked on in a daze. I went back to the old apartment and took some food and some water and one of my cuddly toys. I left because my Dad's body was still there and it frightened me. I never looked back – I just walked away from my previous life. The rioting continued all that second day and as I wandered round hiding and watching I never once saw a policeman. On the third day Russian soldiers at last appeared on the streets and the killing and looting was soon over, once they started shooting. Armenians who wanted to leave were escorted to a large Cultural Centre and this was where I found myself at last and was taken in hand by some adults who were managing the orphanage for kids like me with no parents left.

We were carted about all over the place hardly ever staying more than six months in any one place. We were joined by other orphans from other parts of Azerbaijan, but they kept the Sumgait group together. In due course the orphanage was relocated to the first and second floors of a crumbling apartment block in the town of Sushi in Artsakh, after it was captured by the Armenian army in 1992. It was there that my life was changed yet again when I met my friend Hakan. It was there also some years later, when I was sixteen and Hakan was twelve, where I first met Conrad effendi.

Chapter 22

Conrad

I had arranged to stay on for a further week and to join a small group of British tourists who had already spent a week visiting Georgia. They were in a bus which was due to arrive in Yerevan the next day. They were booked into a more modest hotel in Yerevan than the rather superior hotel; in the main Republic Square in which I had been staying. I duly moved out to this hotel which was in a rougher but livelier part of the town.

My room, on the top floor, stared straight out at Mount Ararat – hanging there in the deep blue sky as if unconnected to the earth below. The weather had begun to turn really hot and this made the sight of that snow-capped peak even lovelier. There are throughout the world a number of great world attractions both natural and man-made which sometimes fail to come up to the expectations raised by all the guidebooks and the literary hyperbole.. Sometimes so excessive is the enthusiastic praise that one arrives with a resistance to being over-impressed. But some sights overcome that resistance. One of these for example is the Taj Mahal in Agra. When I first went to see this building I was determined not to accept all the clichés and praise surrounding it. But I had to admit almost immediately that it was truly greater and more perfect than all the photos had been able to show.

Mount Ararat turned out to be like that, greater than the mental image one had before actually seeing it. One doesn't see it all the time – it comes and goes, firstly according to where you are in the city and secondly as the weather changes from day to day, and indeed sometimes from hour to hour.. At its best it is truly magnificent, standing alone and towering above the city and although forty miles away looking impossibly high.

Now that I had moved to a new hotel in a new area, I had to learn the new minibus routes all over again. I found an infallible way of at least always being able to get back to the hotel wherever I found myself in my wanderings. I chose a suitable outdoor café near the hotel – ordered my 'haygagan sourdj' and sat there noting the number of every minibus that passed by. In the end I had about 20 numbers. Wherever I ended up in the town I needed only to hop onto one of those numbers to know that I would eventually get back. As the fare was fixed however far or little you went it didn't even matter if the line went all over the place before you arrived. Of course one soon learnt the most direct routes.

"Haygagan sourdj" translates as 'Armenian coffee'. This is basically what a European thinks of as 'Turkish coffee'. But rather like in Greece, where you must ask for 'Greek coffee' not Turkish, the same principle applies here. The irony is that this form of coffee drinking was unquestionably introduced to the world by the Ottomans and spread as a result of the Empire.

The British tourist party of about 15 people turned up the next day. A group of all ages including a student of 19 at one end and a retired business man of 75 at the other. Most were Armenians, but there was an architect who had come to study the churches who was Indian, a solicitor who was English and also a BBC producer who was a Scot.

After they had settled in they spent the rest of the day being taken round Yerevan. I did not join them. On the following day we all set off for Gyumri and Spitak. It was a particularly beautiful day, quite different to the rather gloomy journey of the previous week. Gyumri, however, looked only a little better in the sunshine. We moved on to the devastated Spitak, where the group organisers had arranged a viewing of the apartment blocks which the British were funding, to be followed by a banquet in a local restaurant to which they had also invited five of the workers from Spitak who were working on the project, together with the foreman and the architect from Yerevan.

After viewing the apartment blocks we all repaired to the restaurant where the food was already laid out. It started at about 2.30pm. The drink available was vodka as well as wine. The atmosphere lightened up as the food began circulating and the drink began flowing. The Armenian/Caucasian tradition of toasting and speechifying began to pervade the party.

First we drank to each other – the locals toasting all aspects of the English they could think of, and the English toasting everything possible to do with Spitak. Then we all began drinking to various aspects of Armenianness. This was the nationalistic phase and went on for ever until we all lost the capacity to think of anything new in this field. Eventually as we (or at least the men – the ladies were a little more careful) became more and more maudlin (such a nicer word than tipsy) it began to be philosophic concepts like 'love' or 'friendship –the Armenian 'ser'.

I recall, somewhat blurrily, that at one point I became aware of the two buxom and very attractive ladies who owned the restaurant and who had been expertly changing plates and dishes and continually replenishing the vodka whilst avoiding the waving arms of the tipsy speechifying males. Having by then exhausted all the toasts I could think of I found myself toasting 'the cookers'. This was supposed to refer to the two ladies who cooked and served this meal. But my poor Armenian linguistic skills produced the word for 'cooker' – the kitchen appliance. In true Armenian style I then launched into a speech about the reality of 'cookers' and those women who work on whilst the men talked. I knew even as I spoke what a load of rubbish it all was. But the beauty of this whole tradition is that no one really listens anyway. When it finally became clear what I really meant by the word 'cooker' everybody cheered and toasted the two ladies, who grinned back at us though unlikely to have understood what we were saying.

This then started off a spate of toasts to all the ladies present with flowery and rather absurd compliments. The vodka never stopped coming onto the table in large cutglass jugs. One of the English party was a well-respected London solicitor who was an Englishman, who had an Armenian wife. Over the years he had learned Armenian and spoke it well. At the other end of the table was one of the Spitaki workers whose job would be best described as Works Foreman. Both these two gentlemen were portly figures and had clearly taken a shine to each other. Our Armenian foreman had discovered that the name of his new bosom pal was 'Keith'. As usual having difficulty with the 'th' sound this came out as 'Kit'. He would stand up and bellow out "Kit-djan a toast" 'Djan is simply a diminutive endearment – but 'kit' means 'nose in Armenian so he would be bellowing out 'my dear nose' to his new friend.

This would then result in guffaws from the Armenians and redouble the consumption of the vodka. By now it was nearly 6.30 and we had been at it for four hours. The senior engineer then rose to give us what he hoped was to be the final toast. This was to "our dear English friends who sadly now have a long journey back to Yerevan and therefore have to leave, but whom we will miss and always...etc ...etc. However, Kit and his portly and now very flushed friend were having none of it. The toasts flowed on as did the vodka and the ;party broke up only when at last, overcome by sentimental 'ser,' this important London solicitor clumped round the table and our two friends fell into each other's arms swearing eternal friendship.

I doubt if they will ever see each other ever again.

The goodbyes and expressions of perpetual Anglo-Armenian friendship then took another half hour. We drove out of Spitak about 7.30, five hours after we had first sat down to lunch.

The next day we attended an open-air concert held in the countryside to commemorate the battle of Sard-arabad – another glorious nation-state battle not much different to all the other myriad national battles which mean so much to the adolescent boys of the nation-state in question. The dusty road leading from the main road to the site of the concert was lined by a mass of cars and decrepit hired buses, as there was no other means of transport from Yerevan. The great and the good, consisting of the Yerevan big shots together with the wealthier be-suited diaspora smoothies and their wives all had seats in the middle. Everyone else was crowded standing round the edges, or unable to squeeze in at all were sitting on the surrounding grass, smoking and dinking coffee and listening to the music.

Before walking up to the site I had watched a party of Russian soldiers, looking with their fair skins and anxious blue eyes quite impossibly young. They were being taken round by an Armenian army captain. In a field alongside and shaded by two large walnut trees a small group of local mothers were laying out a picnic for a group of the local village kids – obviously their neighbours' kids as well as their own. The children themselves, eight to eleven year olds, and for once mainly boys, were running round kicking a football and quite properly not making the slightest attempt to help their mums. I caught a glimpse of several of the Russian soldiers with a homesick look in their eyes as they passed and watched out of the corner of their eyes the mothers laying out fruit bread and sausage, clearly preferring to be playing football with the other kids rather than going to visit the museum to which they were headed.

However for a Russian boy, a posting during his national; service to the 30,000 strong Russian presence in Armenia must constitute one of the easier and pleasanter postings. Their presence is purely nominal, intended only to make sure that a Russian soldier would have to die if Turkey ever invaded.

When I got up to the concert site I contemplated all those wealthy Westerners sitting plumply in their privileged seats, whilst standing all around were the locals many of whom clearly had children or relatives taking part in the concert. Not once did I hear even a murmur of resentment at the way their concert had been taken over by the great and the good. The moment one of the fat cats had had enough and vacated their seat a couple of kids – a sister and her little brother say, would be pushed forward to take their vacant place, wide-eyed with anticipatory joy.

When it was time to go, the crowd melted away down the road. For a people of such rugged individualists they are remarkably well-disciplined in a crowd. In 1989, just before the break-up of the Soviet Union, Yerevan saw an anti-Soviet demonstration of over one million people. This was the largest anti-Communist demonstration ever to have taken place in the history of the Soviets, and throughout the event there was not a single policeman officially present and not a single life was lost nor a single window broken.

Chapter 23

Conrad in Artsakh

The trip to Nagorno-Karabagh was perhaps the most confusing of all the contrasting images that I had to face in my exploration of the Republic of Armenia. Nagorno-Karabagh is a totally made-up name comprising three languages. 'Bagh' means garden in Persian – 'Kara' is the Turkish word for 'black' – whilst 'Nagorno' is the Russian for 'mountainous'. The whole thing is a Tsarist mish-mash describing a very specific area of the Caucasus. Over the centuries the Armenians have always called the area Artsakh.

During the Tsarist period the South Caucasus – known to the Russians, who of course were looking at it from the other side of the mountains as it were, as the Transcaucasus, was a single administrative area divided into four 'oblasts.' These were run from Tiflis, Yerevan, Baku and Elizavetopol, now know as Gyumri.. It is said that throughout the whole of the Caucasus, north and south of the miountain range, there are about forty separate languages – not dialects, but separate languages. However the three dominant races of the area were the Georgians, the Armenians and the Azeris.

On the fall of the Tsarist regime the area ended up eventually as three separate republics without very clear boundaries but roughly following the three tsarist oblasts. But from the start, Artsakh being part of the fourth hybrid oblast of Elisavetopol was like a Kashmir in the Caucasus and was a cause of war between the new Armenian Republic and Azerbaijan. This war was shortlived, as into the maelstrom arrived the rejuvenated Russians under the Bolshevik regime, who began their reconquest by capturing Baku and suppressing an independent Azerbaijan. They then went on to the suppression of both the republics of Georgia and Armenia.

Stalin was Commissar for the nationalities at the time and he reflected fairly faithfully the early Bolshevik view that 'nationalism' of the traditional 19th century variety was, or at least should be, dead. Lenin genuinely deeply despised all aspects of nationalism. He sincerely believed that this was a totally misguided and irrational emotion. Just as he believed that religion was a fantasy invented by priests and used by the ruling classes to control the masses, so in the same way he felt that worship of the nation-state was equally a fantasy, created in this case by teachers and academics in particular, which was used to exercise and excite the masses whenever their leaders required it in order to distract them from their lowly living conditions. In the last resort, for the sincere Bolshevik the issue was a boring one, upon which he did not want to spend much time or energy. Accordingly, in the end the final territorial settlement within the Soviet empire was in some ways a deliberate mess worked out by a coterie of local Communist leaders who in any case did not think it was important.

In the event, because Stalin and the local Communist leaders, Armenian Communists as well as others, viewed the Armenians as the people most likely to give trouble to the new regime, Soviet Armenia was reduced to its minimum possible size. Artsakh, with its mainly Armenian population was left as an autonomous province of the new Soviet republic of Azerbaijan. So matters stood until the fall of the Soviet Empire in 1991. Then the Armenians of Artsakh revolted and demanded to become part of independent Armenia. As if the Soviet empire had never existed at all, the new republics of Armenia and Azerbaijan took up a new war almost exactly where they had left off 70 years before. This time, however, for various reasons the Armenians were totally victorious militarily, and the Armenian army not only occupied Artsakh but also put under occupation a significant part of Azerbaijan lying between Artsakh proper and Armenia.

The south-western tip of Artsakh comes within a few miles as the crow flies of a corner of Armenia. This is however across a deep ravine through which flows the river Hakari and which ravine the Bolsheviks had left as part of Azerbaijan. A cease-fire was negotiated in 1994 putting all this area under Armenian control- and this has remained the position even after a further five years. A modern road, financed by the diaspora, has been constructed winding its way down from the empty Armenian highlands on one side, across the river on a new bridge, through the half abandoned town of Lachin (now renamed Berdzor), and up to the equally empty Artsakh highlands on the other side and on to Stepanakert, the capital.

Like any other Armenian I felt happy that the Armenians of Artsakh, long abandoned by everyone had at last de facto if not de jure joined up with their fellow countrymen. It was as much a source of pride that Armenian discipline and military expertise had won such a clear-cut victory over old enemies, as the pride created by say John of Gaunt's speech,. On the other hand ethnic cleansing, wherever it is done and however historically justified it might seem to be, is a twentieth century phenomenon which is a terrible reflection on our society. Villages that had lived side by side for centuries suddenly had to be abandoned by one side or the other. Azeri villagers fleeing from the Artsakh countryside, and Armenian suburbanites of Baku uprooting themselves and abandoning houses lived in by generations of their ancestors.

As we drove further from Yerevan, and as we got closer to Artsakh the villages got fewer and poorer and the mountains and the passes got higher and higher. We only once saw any evidence of the Army. We had stopped and were having a sort of picnic on the grass next to one of the delightful rivers rushing turbulently along. We were passed by a platoon of Armenian soldiers who were on a route march. They were all very young, but all smiled and bantered with the ladies in our group. Both sides were openly curious about each other and they did not mind at all being photographed by our ladies to whom they each gave a friendly wave.

The road got worse and worse and the countryside more and more deserted until we at last came upon the old frontier post. Here the new road started weaving its way down into the Hakari valley. Looking across the ravine to Artsakh at the same height on the other side there was no sign of any further human habitation – though the scenery, fully wooded on the other side, was stunning.

My mind went to Hamlet's lines when he sees Fortinbras' army passing in front of him marching to fight for a few square miles of land in Poland. I could not remember the actual words, but the soldier to whom he asks for information tells him that they are all off to fight for some land with no value and which no farmer would deign to cultivate, and for which he himself would not give a few shillings. Hamlet's reply is to the effect – "Well, the Polack will not defend it then". Whereupon the soldier assures him that the Polack would certainly defend it and had already garrisoned it and was waiting to fight the mother of battles for it.

We had in our party a school teacher who evinced a great enthusiasm for military victory so long of course that it was hers – who quoted patriotic songs and poems and who assured me that there was no comparison whatsoever between the dynastic quarrels of the Danish and Polish Royal families in the fifteenth century - and what the Republic of Armenia had fought for. Well perhaps so, but then Orwell's dictum, expanded to take in this situation, comes uncomfortably to mind.

Anyway down to the river Hakari we went and across a bridge reputedly built at the cost of a million dollars and came up to the former village of Lachin, the battle for which had cost so many lives on both sides. A mixed town lived in quite amicably in the Soviet era by both communities. Now abandoned by the Azeri population, with over half the houses standing empty and in many cases roofless. The excellent new road, really one of the best we ever drove on throughout our tour, now continued through really spectacular landscape for another twisting fifty kilometres, into one ravine and up and over into another. The mountains, unlike those in Armenia, were covered with thick lush and dense forests and the whole countryside is beautiful. But there were no villages, no people and no traffic on the beautifully engineered road, which was a political statement rather than an economic requirement. We arrived in Stepanakert – the capital – a wholly Armenian town and which had always been wholly Armenian.

Our second day in Artsakh dawned magnificently with a bright sun and beautiful blue skies. The view from our hotel, owned and managed by three Australian businessmen, was superb. Forested mountains; bright green hillside meadows; rivers that twinkled along; and above all none of the Soviet industrial detritus that so mars Armenia itself! Could it be after all that it was worth fighting for? Nonsense! Beauty is beauty and can be appreciated by everyone regardless of which particular nation-state owns it. If tomorrow Scotland became an independent sovereign nation-state, would it make the Highland scenery somehow less appealing to an English visitor.

The next day we drove off into the country to visit one of Artsakh's hilltop monasteries – Gandsazar. The landscape was truly spectacular. The area has a quite breathtaking though undramatic beauty, together with an extraordinary clarity of the air which allows you to see for miles. We turned off the main road and bumped along a country road, eventually reaching the little town of Vank. Here we began a hairy ascent up a one-track dirt road clinging to the side of the mountain and with a sheer drop on one side. The whole hillside was covered with small trees, green meadows with wild flowers of all kinds and an occasional field of red poppies. Right at the very top, surrounded by a low stone wall stands a wonderful 12th century church. Forming a square with the church, but not connected directly to it are the old monastery buildings.

This is still a functioning monastery, and one of the monks turned up and gently offered to take us round once we were ready and had imbibed the silent peaceful atmosphere. I have never met such a sweet and gentle cleric. He stood patiently at the door of the church waiting whilst we wandered round taking in the views, the sculptures and the sheer longevity of the site. When we were ready he took us round the church and also into one of the cells – I presumed his own.

This was a spot to linger and reflect. As I was sitting in the courtyard in the shade of a large tree, talking with our driver who was a local, and who was driving us in place of our regular driver to give him a day free, there was some gunfire in the woods surrounding the monastery. Our driver who was from the village of Vank that we had driven through on our way up commented that five years before, during the Armeno-Azeri war, gunfire like that would not be men out hunting and would be met by the young men going out to hunt whoever was doing the shooting, while the women and children went in and bolted the doors. He then went on to tell me about our gentle priest – Der Hovnan – who had been showing us around.

During the early stages of the war before the intervention of the Armenian army, the Azeris tried to capture this monastery. There were periodic air strikes aimed at destroying it, which did indeed do some damage. There was also an infantry attempt to take the hill complex. The local villagers from Vank, of whom Hovnan was one, formed themselves into volunteer bands, operating from the village and the surrounding woods in order to defend the monastery.. They had few weapons to begin with. It appears that Hovnan, who one could see was a big strong man, killed at least five men in the course of this fighting – and without any modern weapons. Eventually as the villagers began to capture more and more Azeri weapons, the Azeris were defeated and melted away. Apparently, when the war ended – five years ago now – Hovnan could not rid himself of the guilt over the deaths he had caused directly and face to face. The memories haunted him, and eventually he joined the monastery and became a novitiate priest. Believe me you could not have met a more gentle, cheerful and patient a man.

Eventually we were rounded up by our driver and left. But first a car was sent down the track to make sure the road was clear, and to stop any approaching cars at the bottom of the hill till we had passed. There was literally nowhere along the track where two cars let alone a minibus could pass each other. That afternoon we stopped for lunch at an open-air spot. The only indication that there was someone prepared to give us some simple food was a battered old barbecue smoking away at the side of the road, from which nevertheless, within fifteen minutes after we stopped, came some delicious kebabs which we ate sitting on the grass straight from the skewers.

Chapter 24

Hakan

I never knew my father. When I was really little I simply thought that I had never had one. Of course as I grew older and first went to school I came to realise that my mother Miriam lived in some sort of disgrace – a disgrace that was, it seemed, all due to me and to the fact that I had no father. When the war broke out against the Armenians, my mother and I were living in the basement of one of the big apartment blocks in Shusha. We were of course in the Azeri quarter, but on the edge. The apartment blocks on the other side of the street were Armenian. I was only four when the conflict broke out.

I was mercilessly teased and bullied when I started going to school but at least those school experiences gave me some idea of the reason that I had no family apart from my mother. – she herself never told me anything about her past. To this day I am, not too sure how we lived and where my mother got her money from. As I grew older after the catastrophe, I came to realise where our money must have come from – but I cannot recall ever having seen any strange men in our little basement apartment.

When the war started I noticed that all our Armenian neighbours on the other side of the street had fled or been forced to leave. Even at that young age I knew that Armenians were different from me and the other boys in my school – but I did not know how or why.. I was told by one of the boys in our little school, no older than me, that they worshipped three Gods, whereas I did know that we worshipped only one. The school to which my mother sent me was a sort of private establishment where we all sat in front of a teacher and recited verses in a language I didn't understand. My mother must have paid for me to attend this place, but I had no idea what I was supposed to be learning. I had no friends, no cousins, no family to tell me what it was all about. My mother would never talk to me –I don't think that she liked me. I desperately wanted to have a father or an elder brother or someone I could talk to who could explain things to me. All the teacher ever did was to rap us over the head or the shoulder with a long cane if we got the verses wrong, or started staring out of the window.

I was teased about things that I scarcely understood, and the bigger boys who were about to go on to a proper school would push me around when we went out to play in the courtyard. Eventually, without saying a word to my mother, I stopped going to this odd establishment. I would set off in the morning with my piece of pitta and an onion or tomato or whatever in my satchel – but would stroll elsewhere rather than go to school. I would wander round the town and go and watch the soldiers as they bombarded the Armenian town which was below us in the valley. I had no idea then, but later heard that it was called Stepanakert – and that many of the neighbours who had fled from our town had ended up there.

It was very exciting though again I had no idea what it was all about. In any case it was better than sitting in that dingy school room and being bullied in the playground. The soldiers were in a sort of pit surrounded by sandbags and which had a piece of artillery in it. This fired up into the air but I could see that the shell went down into the town below. As I was there so often sitting on the grass and watching, one or two of the soldiers began to notice me. They found out my name and would call out –

"Hey Hakan – what have you got for us?"

I would offer them whatever my mother had packed for my lunch – but they would laugh and make me come and sit with them while they ate their own lunch. For these few weeks I was, I think, happy for the first time. This must be like having family – friendship which I had never experienced before. It was male and it was what I imagined having a father would have been like.

I was five years old when the Armenians mounted their attack on the town. Until then the Armenians had not entered my conscious thoughts. They were simply 'the enemy down there in the valley' and they were a few miles away.. I didn't even equate them with the previous neighbours who had lived in the Armenian blocks just across the street from us. I don't think that I even thought of them as people at all. They were like the comic-book baddies which I had seen, before I stopped going, in the comics owned by some of the boys at the little school.

I was squatting near one of my favourite sandbagged redoubts early in the morning when a tremendous bombardment – against us – against us – started. There was a lot of noise, smoke everywhere and then gunshots coming out of the morning mist drifting up below us. This was war at last. Until then I really had had no idea what war meant. I was terrified and had no idea what to do. I crept behind a stone wall. The bombardment seemed to go on for ever. Then as the mist and smoke began to clear I saw some soldiers advancing up the hill towards us, still quite far away. They didn't look all that much different from the soldiers in the redoubt with whom I had become so friendly.

I was sort of transfixed by what I was seeing, but then I saw one of the soldiers in the redoubt crouching behind the parapet get shot, and I saw him stagger back and fall down bleeding. The sight of the blood and the screams and shouts brought me back to my senses. My terror returned and I'm afraid I peed a bit in my pants. I turned and running along the wall I worked my way back into the town centre. Here there was a lot of panic with women and children running about, some of them screaming. I made a bee-line to our apartment block. It had already received a direct hit from some shells and some of the upper storeys were ruined, but I had no difficulty in getting down the stairs to our basement rooms.

My mother was not there.

I had no idea where she might be. I cowered in a corner all the rest of the day and the night listening to the sounds of guns all around. My mother never returned. I never ever saw her again. I don't think that she was killed – I discovered later that there were very few civilian casualties – I think she just disappeared with all the other Azeri women and children who fled or were escorted out in groups to other parts of the country. I have no real idea what could have happened, but I suspect that she was quite glad to be rid of me. The next morning I crept out, but then, the moment I got out of the front door of the crumbling building in order to look out and find out what was going on, there was a huge, a massive, explosion. I saw down the hillside not that far away a large part of the Armenian Cathedral blow up. I am 12 years old now but then I was only 5. I peed in my pants again – and this time not just a few drops. I ran back into our little rooms, and this time I stayed put for the next few days.

After a few days of cowering in the basement I eventually had to creep out again. I was used to wandering round the town on my own from all those days that I had been avoiding school. The town was in a state of total confusion. There were Armenian soldiers everywhere. They were not harassing the inhabitants – at this stage still all Azeris. The Azeri inhabitants were all packing up and leaving in droves. Nevertheless as they fled – I don't know where they went to – Armenian soldiers began looting the apartments as they emptied. Day by day the town began to take on a devastated and desolate appearance. All the people who had lived around us departed, at first in hordes, but then in trickles of those who were left. Once they were all gone, most of the Armenian soldiers also left, leaving only a small garrison. These few soldiers manned the walls and took over the old redoubts that I used to visit when they were manned by Azeri soldiers.

I already knew quite a bit of Armenian chatting with other boys in the streets before the war began. I quickly picked up more as slowly more and more Armenian families, refugees from other parts of the country came in and moved into the more habitable empty apartments. For quite a long time I managed to get by, by stealing food from the empty apartments, and by doing odd errands for people, but then I made friends with some of the Armenian soldiers manning the same redoubts that had previously been manned by the Azeris. They even called out to me when I would arrive at lunchtime –

"Hey Hakan – what have you got for us?"

I occasionally had some sweets or some sticky cake which I had earned or stolen and which I would share with them – but more often, in fact almost every day, it was they who gave me food from their own lunch packs.

After a further year, as the fighting died down, more and more Armenian families drifted in and took up residence in some of the empty blocks that were still relatively unscathed. I discovered that most of them were from parts of Azerbaijan where they had been forced out of their homes in the same way as had happened here the other way round. My own apartment block had no roof and remained completely empty for some time. Then one day two large lorries drove up and deposited a whole lot of boys of all ages from 8 upwards. With them were some adults, clearly in charge. They took over all the apartments on the 1st and 2nd floors of the building – which were the least damaged, and I heard a lot of banging and noise of building for the next few weeks.

I became more careful in my comings and goings as I didn't want to be seen too much. However, my Armenian had become completely fluent and when I was occasionally accosted it was easy for me to deal with any questions as to my identity. Even though it was almost five years since I started living alone I had not entirely forgotten my Azeri and could occasionally speak it with the one or two old men who had elected to remain, after the town hade fallen to the Armenians..

I was 10 years old, completely uneducated, unable to read or write in either language, when I first met Razmik. He was exploring the building one afternoon after coming home from school. He spotted me creeping in and going down the increasingly disintegrating stairs to the basement. He was 14 years old, tall and manly. He had started shaving and I thought he was older. He followed me downstairs and came straight in to our basement flat without knocking. We started chatting. I told him that I was born in Sushi. He assumed, to begin with, that I was an Armenian left over from when the Armenians fled the city at the start of the war. But my name was Hakan – that's a Moslem name – I was not prepared to deny my name. So that very first afternoon

I ended up telling him all my history.

From that day on Razmik began coming to my two little rooms every day after school – and I for my part began making sure that I was always home by then. He began taking food from the orphanage kitchen whenever he could and brining it down for us in the evenings. Eventually the day came when he discovered that I was completely unregistered and that I had never been to a proper school. He began shouting and insisting that I had to start going to school, at least to learn to read and write. But I didn't dare approach any authority – how after all could I explain myself. In the end Razmik said he would teach me himself. Many of the other boys in the orphanage were already working on jobs in the town and staying away till late at night and so Razmik was not missed. He brought exercise books and pens and paper from his own school, and we spent hours at my kitchen table as he patiently taught me the alphabet, and we began reading together.

On one occasion, after about a year had gone by, I was just eleven and I suppose Razmik was fifteen, when he suggested that he would take off the whole afternoon from school to come and be with me at lunchtime. We had planned to have lunch together and do some reading. I have to admit that I totally forgot about it and had gone down to chat with the soldiers as I used to do. For some time they had taught me to smoke, and we used to smoke together, but I had promised Razmik that I wouldn't anymore. Well he guessed where I was and came storming down and saw me smoking as well. He wouldn't shame me in front of the soldiers, but I followed meekly enough. He was very angry and when we got home, he gave me a smack on the back of my bare legs. I said I was sorry and we ate lunch in silence – but afterwards we read together and he forgot it all and gave me a hug before going up to bed, though he did again make me promise not to smoke anymore.

But I didn't forget it. This was what it must mean to have a father; to have someone who cared for you to that extent. He was the only male role model I had ever had. I loved him.

The moment arrived when Razmik had to leave the orphanage. I myself was now over 12 and could read and write. Indeed I had become an avid reader, trying to make up for all those lost years. Razmik did get a job in the booming construction sector. I too found a job – delivering milk and other groceries from a shop to customers who did not want to take them up all those stairs – hardly any lifts in the town worked at all. Razmik now turned sixteen and had to leave the orphanage and find somewhere else to live. There was still a lot of empty accommodation all over the town, and eventually he did get hold of an apartment in one of the empty blocks in the old Azeri quarter.

I remember with joy his words one evening when I got back from my own work and sat waiting for him. Razmik came bursting in and said –

"Hakan, I've found a flat. It's got running water, but no electricity as yet. Will you come and share with me. We can take your bed, and this table and the chairs to get us started."

I could not contain my glee. I jumped up and ran to hug him. I was getting taller myself and I leant up and gave him a kiss on his cheek. I sought to move from his cheek and kiss him again on the lips – my only family – but he recoiled, simply kissing me back on my forehead.

Chapter 25

Conrad

For our last day in Artsakh the arrangement was that we were to visit the town of Sushi, a few miles up the mountainside. This is a very old town strategically placed near the top of a mountain right above Stepanakert and with commanding views over the whole main valley. Whereas most of the rest of Artsakh was populated solely by Armenians, Sushi was a mixed Armeno-Azeri town with an accepted significant preponderance of Azeris. There were two or three mosques and only one church.

As the war had intensified, the Armenians in the town had fled to Stepanakert, five miles away down the mountainside. The Azeris dumped all their ammunition in the Church and began lobbing shells onto the villages and the city in the valley below. Sushi is a natural strategic town. Some of the walls, originally built to withstand a Mongol attempt to take the area in the 13th century, are still standing. This defence constituted one of the few defeats suffered by those early Mongol invaders – they never in fact took Sushi. The local Armenians, having fled and now hiding out in Stepanakert, were now backed by the Armenian army and felt they were in a position to retake the town. They trained themselves with regular army help and duly mounted an assault on the town. In the course of the assault, on the second day of the offensive, the church blew up in a massive explosion due to all the ammunition being stored there. It is a totally fruitless exercise and a pointlessly everlasting argument to explore whose fault it was. Either way, the town fell and the Azeri occupants now fled in their turn.

Today it remains a sad town. Ethnic cleansing, of which ironically the Armenians were the first victims of the twentieth century, is never a pretty sight whoever is the victim. It always seems to involve the burning or removing of the roofs of the houses of the displaced people. Great swathes of the town are empty of people, with streets of abandoned houses and burnt-out blocks of flats. The only part of the church which had been left standing was the main entrance and the belfry tower. I should add that one of the mosques is a total ruin, while the other two are in a state of decay and parts of the minaret have already fallen. The remaining people in the town, now almost entirely Armenians, look some-how lost – although as usual the children who gathered around us as we walked through the town were lively and curious. They always picked out our portly and red-faced London solicitor as being more 'odar'(foreign) than the rest of us and were always absolutely delight-ed, though remaining shy and tongue-tied, when he ad-dressed them In excellent if accented Armenian, after first confirming to the original questioning that he was indeed not Armenian.

However, Sushi brought back many of my old doubts all over again – and that was even before I met Raz-mik and Hakan. There was a triumphalist spirit in most of our party – particularly our academics – which dis-turbed me. Furthermore there was a clear difference between this group of diaspora Armenians bursting to feel pride in their countrymen's success , and the local Sushi Armenians who without a doubt had a sad and slightly lost look.

I was sitting in the square outside the ruined cathe-dral on my own fiddling with my camera when these two young boys came up to me. They asked if I could take a picture of them together. I assumed that they were brothers, although even then I noticed that the older one with his fair skin, long face and brown eyes looked clearly Armenian while the young one was more like me with darker features. They were delighted by the picture-taking and quite spontaneously invited me to come home with them and see their apartment. I went off with them with great anticipatory pleasure, as seeing people and talking with them in the streets is not at all like visiting them in their homes.

Their apartment was in a ruined block in the old Azeri quarter. They were clearly immensely proud of it. It was very sparsely furnished. There were no easy chairs but there was a good kitchen table and we sat round it having innumerable cups of tea which was served by the youngest of the boys who kept filling up our tiny cups from a kettle being boiled over a paraffin hob. The eldest boy was almost a young man. His name was Razmik and he came from Sumgait. He told me his story and how he had eventually ended up here in Sushi. I asked him if he hated Azeris as a result of how he had been treated in Sumgait. He was quite clear that he refused to equate all Azeris with the inflamed mobs he had been forced to watch in Sumgait.

"But you had to watch them raping your mother," I said, "and they were all Azeris."

"Of course I hated them – and still do," he answered " but suppose all of them were redheaded, would it be logical for me then to hate all red-headed people."

Of course I was impressed by what seemed to me to be a great maturity in one so young – he was after all only 16. But I couldn't entirely believe it. Perhaps he had somehow picked up something of my own feelings about nationalist fervour and was hiding his true feelings.

"Come" I said, " it's not quite the same thing – having

red hair might admittedly be one of a rapists' identifying characteristics, but it cannot compare in importance with his national identity."

"What is so important about 'national identity'. What am I then, with an Armenian father and a Georgian mother born and living in Azerbaijan?"

"No...no, its not that difficult – you chose, or rather your parents chose to bring you up as Armenian. You went to an Armenian school, your friends were Armenian, you spoke Armenian as your first language. It is culture that counts not birth genetics."

"But sir that still does not explain why I should hate Azeris. I love Hakan, and his being Azeri makes not the slightest difference to that.....either way."

I felt entirely humbled by that, having started from the premiss that after all that experience he had to detest all Azeris. I turned to Hakan as he filled my ever-weakening cup of tea with more hot water and asked to hear his story. After hearing him out it all seemed clear – the one factor which did not count in either of their stories was their national identity. I wondered how the nation-state fanatics would deal with that – I suppose they would say that this was the exception. My feeling was that whilst it may be exceptional in areas where there was no mixed ethnicity - it would not be so in areas where there was no such uniformity. My mind went to the situation of mixed marriages in the former Yugoslavia.

I adored these kids and wanted to investigate more. I told them that I would give them my camera if they would write their stories down for me. Just an hour I said. Hakan was not too sure that he could manage, but Razmik was very keen as he eyed my state of the art camera and told Hakan that he would help him. But when could they give it to me and when could I give them the camera. It was Hakan who then suggested that I stay the night with them and share their dinner. I pointed out that my party was leaving for Yerevan the next day. He was quick to point out that there were now several taxis in Shushi and I could get one in the morning – he himself would run round at once and order one for early the next morning.

What a chance – I left them sitting at the table working at their stories and went down to my group who were just collecting at the minibus. I told them that I was staying the night, but that I would be with them when our bus was due to leave to return to Yerevan the next day. I should explain that it was a Sunday and neither of the boys were working.

It turned out to be a delightful evening. I sent Hakan out to get some kebabs and some fresh fruit – all the kebabjis were open, but getting the fresh fruit was a bit more difficult. The boys finished their stories and I put the precious folios in my rucksack. We spent a lot of the evening, entirely in candlelight as there was no electricity in the apartment, with me showing them how the camera worked. We then had the drama of where I was to sleep. I was quite happy to sleep in the main room on the floor over a few blankets. Razmik was quite happy with that, but Hakan would have none of it. He absolutely insisted that I should sleep in his bed and that he would sleep with Razmik. He kept shaming Razmik saying that there was no way Caucasian hospitality, whether Armenian, Georgian or Azeri could allow a guest to sleep on the floor.

There were wheels within wheels in the argument. It didn't go on for long, as Hakan easily prevailed – but it became clear to me that poor Hakan wanted to sleep with Razmik. I suspect that he had done so when they were both younger. He was only twelve and I don't think there was the slightest element of anything sexual in what he wanted. He was desperate for a father figure or the love of an elder brother, whereas Razmik at 16 was worried in case his love for the younger boy might turn into what for him would be shameful. I don't know how it would turn out in the end and I never did ever know.

I went down by taxi to Stepanakert the next morning and we all left for Yerevan on the long bus journey back through Lachin and across the Hakari bridge. The first thing I heard when I got back in the evening was a telegram sent by my son telling me that Harriet had had a second stroke and was now completely paralysed. Everything changed and I immediately took a flight back to London. I never heard from the two boys ever again, as all the issues surrounding Harriet's condition took over my life. However the memory of Razmik's refusal to commit himself to a hatred of a class, refusing to succumb to an easy acceptance of a belief in a collective guilt for people who had harmed him, remained with me for the rest of my life.

I arrived back in London the next day and from that moment there was no more consideration of abstract matters like personal identity issues. Poor Harriet's condition was terrible. For some weeks she remained in hospital, but as the days went by it became clear that she could never be cured and would soon have to come home and the rest of the summer was spent in dealing with the physical arrangements that had to be made.

The bombshell caused by Harriet's decision to seek the help of Dignitas was then the subject of hours upon hours of argument and discussion within the family. By the end of 1999, however, I was satisfied that she meant what she wanted and was clear in her mind. I decided to fulfil my original promise to her and agreed to drive her to Switzerland. It was going to be difficult – and by that I mean the sheer physical problem of getting her into cars and out into hotels. Conradin immediately offered to come with me and help, but I declined any help from anybody in the family, in view of William's warnings about the state of the law on the matter. In the end – with the help of Dignitas itself, I arranged for a Nurse to be employed to meet me in Calais and come with us on our last journey. Mercifully she did not speak English and Harriet and I were able to have our last talks together in the car as the hired nurse slept in the back.

Chapter 26

Charles

After I had prepared my own report, concentrating on the relationship which I had established that existed between Bridgeman and his wife, I delivered it to all the other members of the Committee of the CPS which was investigating the Bridgeman problem. There was clearly no great hurry. So far, this was the first case which had come to our attention. The Committee had even agreed that there was no harm in Conrad keeping his passport and being allowed to go abroad if he wanted. After all he had returned from Switzerland after the assisted suicide of his wife and had agreed to be arrested on his return. This was still early days in the formation of Dignitas and neither we nor the police were aware of any other British citizens taking advantage of the Dignitas offer of assisted suicide.

As all the reports came in and were distributed we decided that we needed one full days deliberation when each of us would formally introduce our individual reports, and then discuss together all the issues. It is of course impossible for me to disclose the names of the members who put forward their views, so I will have to resort to Mr.A. and Sir B. but it is important to remember that they were not abstract figures – they each had their own personalities which influenced their decisions. For a start, Mr.A. was adamant that we had to get a bit of a move on, because we had to be in a position to be clear ourselves about what we at least believed the law actually meant, in case we had to face a flood.

We started by looking again at exactly what it was that Dignitas offered, and what would have taken place when Harriet Bridgeman was brought in, in her wheel-chair. It was quite clear from the Dignitas information sheets what was supposed to happen and we had no need to ascertain whether exactly the same procedure was followed in her case. Mr. A. backed by Sir G. took the line that it was all in any case pretty irrelevant. What was to be decided here was English Law, not Swiss. However the general feeling was that for a clear deci-sion we had to take into account what had actually taken place in that clinic in Zurich.

After going through all the reports the only Doctor in our group – a Dr.F. - spoke about people being afraid of finding themselves in some sort of helpless condi-tion – of being conscious but unable to do or say any-thing, tied to some machine being kept artificially alive by state-of-the-art medical technology. He quoted the saying – "people want to give meaningful life to their last years, not meaningless years to their life.". I found myself agreeing and thought I knew which way he was going to vote. But as it happens I was wrong.

Mr. A. now intervened and insisted we look at the matter simply on the same basis as any other criminal prosecution. First, what was the current law on the sub-ject at issue; then a simple matter of did the defendant's actions breach that law; finally do we have enough evi-dence to prosecute. Looking round at us all and speak-ing very clearly he said –

"Clearly there is no issue of evidence here and there never will be in view of the frankness in which all the Bridgeman family have talked to us and to the Police. So, it is simply a matter of what is the law. Well the law is for once crystal clear. In England and Wales it is completely unambiguous that it is a criminal offence to encourage or to assist in any suicide or any suicide at-tempt. Actually this does not even require a death – an

201

attempted suicide would be enough. Nor for that matter is the state of mind of Harriet Bridgeman relevant either. Conrad Bridgeman helped his wife into the car, drove her to Zurich, made arrangements to meet people there, wheeled his wife in and was present when she injected herself, or was helped to inject herself, with some sort of lethal poison. Why are you wasting your time considering cultural or religious attitudes to assisted suicide. You have no choice. We must prosecute and we must ask for a custodial sentence."

At this point our chairman intervened –

"Look here, A. don't tell us that it is just a matter of the existing law. There have been innumerable cases where we were all quite clear on the strict rule of the law, but we have decided not to prosecute for some reason of public policy."

"But chairman" intervened Sir G. our resident Christian, "that was usually in cases where the law was clear and where the public had no confusion in its mind, but where there was some special element added to the case to make prosecution not worthwhile. But here we have a situation where the public is, I suspect, not entirely clear where the law stands, and it behoves us to make the law clear by prosecuting. I am not so sure about A's desire for a maximum sentence, but I cannot see how we can shirk our clear duty to recommend a full prosecution."

Others now spoke, although I cannot now recall exactly who said what.

"Sooner or later the media are going to get hold of this problem and the issue is going to go smack-bang into the public arena. We simply cannot dither on the issue any longer."

"Moral scruples is not the problem here. The CPS must be seen to be enforcing the law as it stands now at this exact moment. If the public or the state wants to change the law, that's what Parliament is for. But until that is done our only duty is not to debate the morality or otherwise of Major Bridgeman's actions, but simply to decide whether they were against the law."

There was an immediate rejoinder from the other side of the table-

"Look that's not entirely right. We are not really debating that issue at all. We all of us round this table know perfectly well that this man's actions were against the law. The only issue is whether it is right as a matter of public policy for us to prosecute."

To my surprise Dr.F. now spoke up again and said –

"For heaven's sake we simply must prosecute. We have no choice in the matter. I'm sure you recall the case, was it in the 1930's, when a Doctor performed an abortion on a girl who had been gang-raped by some soldiers. Gosh I am getting old, here am I both a medical man and a lawyer of forty years standing and I can't remember the name of the case" – at which point A. called out the name of the case. F. then continued –

"Well as you recall the girl after becoming pregnant was in a state of frightful psychological trauma. She put her case to the Doctor and told him that she simply could not go through with her pregnancy – she would not even know who would have been the father of any child. She would rather kill herself. The Doctor decided to perform an abortion which was of course entirely illegal at the time, regardless of the period of the pregnancy. He took the line that it was his clinical decision, and that in the end it was an operation required to save his patient's life. He then decided after the successful operation to inform the Police and invite a prosecution."

"Now the reason I am going through all this and I am afraid being rather long-winded about it is to show why in the end I too believe that there should be a prosecution. I cannot remember exactly what happened in that old abortion case, but I believe that in the end the Jury refused to convict, and in the end it forced a change in the law. In the same way a prosecution here could help to clarify the position – for one way or another this situation is not going to go away and we are going to face further such incidents in the future."

Sir G. nodded and then added-

"Today we know of no one else who has wanted to take this route – but who knows in a few years there may be a rush towards this route of despair. I myself believe that suicide is a deep sin – well you would expect me to I suppose. I know, I know, no need to laugh I know that a sin is not necessarily against the law. But as it happens this one is."

"Come," said our chairman, "I think we've looked into all aspects of this now and I have to report to the Director of Public Prosecutions tomorrow. Are we unanimous on this? I seem to sense a consensus in favour of going ahead with a prosecution."

I at last spoke up. My report had been fairly long and conclusive so I had had nothing much to add to the discussions, of which I have only been able to provide a flavour here.

"Mr. Chairman, I have to say that I will have to insist on a vote as I will be voting against any decision to mount a prosecution, If there was ever a case against prosecuting a crime as a matter of public policy this must surely be it. This is one of those grey and difficult areas where Parliament will find it difficult to act. Maybe 100 years ago, before the days of professional politicians, men with spirit and convictions could and did act in moral issues like this without fear – but I suspect that this problem is going to grow and grow and our current legislators, regardless of party or faction, are going to chicken out of doing anything about it, because of worry for their jobs."

"I think that the answer must surely be that so long as there is no selfish motive shown, we should not prosecute. Imagine once we prosecute we will have to keep at it – heaven's our border police might even have to stop invalid's travelling to Switzerland without checking on their motivation.. Gentlemen, it is my belief that if more of our citizens decide to take this route, future Committees of the CPS will not prosecute."

Nobody agreed with me, and after some more comments and in the interest of unanimity I was pressured to withdraw my formal opposition, though I insisted that my objection should be noted on the minutes. Thus it was that by a formally unanimous vote the CPS in the year 2000 decided to prosecute Conrad Bridgeman under Section 2 of the Suicide Act 1961, requiring a maximum penalty of 14 years imprisonment.

Chapter 27

Sima

At no time after he returned from Switzerland did I ever see my father at all concerned or anxious as to whether he would be prosecuted for having helped Harriet to take her own life. He regularly quoted his own father, my grandfather Harry, who had faced a court-martial for having acted on his conscience against the direct orders of a superior officer at the time of the great fire of Smyrna. No, he refused to worry about it for a moment – he was far more interested in the decision by my nephew Conradin to read History at University. Conradin had turned 16 during the previous year and was now approaching 17.

Conradin was a lovely lively boy who got on with everyone except his father – though even some of that was simply teenage angst. He had blue eyes and fair hair and was in a way the least Armenian looking of all the family. Academically he was specialising in the outbreak and origins of the Great War. He was due to submit some sort of paper, or something like that, on the subject as part of a scholarship exam. Well I don't know exactly – neither the actual type of exam nor when or where it was being mounted. My Dad was fascinated. Conrad was fairly knowledgeable about that period, largely because his father had been so closely connected to the naval events at the start of that war. Conradin became a keen visitor to our house as the summer began and he and his grandfather would sit talking about 1914 as if it were yesterday.

Meanwhile I was going out with Charles Tierney almost every day. I couldn't decide whether I was in love with him – but I soon became fairly sure that he loved me. I have been out with other boy-friends whom I have 'fancied,' and who have 'fancied' me – but I have never felt that any of them ever loved me. Charles was different. Not perhaps a great heroic figure – beginning to get a bit plump – but wonderful company. Easy to talk to and with views which almost always coincided with mine. When they didn't, I was beginning to learn not always to want to have the last word.

On the matter of the prosecution of Conrad he was very careful and professional, and we never discussed how the case was progressing. Then, one day, it was a weekend, I spent the whole day and night in his flat – and we ended up discussing the issue which we had been avoiding for weeks. Charles really showed his true feelings for me that afternoon after we had got up from bed to have an early supper. Despite his careful professional reserve which went deep in his training, he told me that the day before, the CPS had decided to start the process of mounting a prosecution. I fully understood right away that I could not say a word to anyone, least of all to Conrad, as even now there might be no case to answer as there was still a lot to do before the proceedings could start. I thrilled to the fact that Charles was willing to show me so much trust. In some ways it meant more to me than all the tenderness and passion of his love-making.

Until the last moment he had himself opposed a prosecution. However, he wanted me to know that while he still did think that it was wrong to prosecute, and that if trips to Switzerland for this purpose became more common, future decisions would be not to prosecute, nevertheless he could not approve of voluntary euthanasia. It was not the religious beliefs of his colleagues, but his worry about the 'slippery slope' argument. Furthermore he was convinced that despite the fact that Conrad had helped Harriet to the death she craved, nevertheless he had had to act against his own convictions as he too was basically against any form of suicide.

I myself had had to witness at first hand, day by day, my mother's suffering. I was therefore fairly clear in my own mind. I told Charles that all people of sound mind should have the freedom of choice as to how they wanted to live their lives. This included the right to control their own body and their own life, so long of course that they didn't infringe anyone else's rights. It followed that if that principle was accepted, the State should not seek to create laws that prevent people from being able to choose how and when they would die. Charles replied, and I will quote him and my replies directly –

"But my darling, it is really not so simple. Leaving aside the religious arguments, there is….."

"What religious arguments?"

"Oh, you know the argument that as it is God who has granted life, only he has the right to end it."

"What about murder?"

"Well there you are that is precisely it. Murder is a sin – and suicide is a form of murder."

"Nonsense – they are not morally equivalent."

"Sima it is not nonsense for some people – but I accept that it is not an argument that would appeal to the likes of us. However, there is an argument which has come to mean a lot more to me. Society must reflect that once a healthcare service, or a government department, or a charitable organisation starts helping to kill its own citizens a line will have been crossed that we may all come to rue in the future. A Society that allows voluntary euthanasia could – and indeed people say inevitably will – gradually change its attitude to include involuntary euthanasia."

"Oh Charles surely not!"

"No Sima, I can see it. For example, with voluntary euthanasia totally legalised and in general use, very ill or terminally ill elderly people who are helpless and need constant care, may feel pressured to request euthanasia in order not to be a burden on their family. It would appear to be voluntary, but it wouldn't be, and that is just the start of a dreadful slippery slope."

"Oh God, Charles, it's a depressing subject. I can see what you are saying and now I am confused all over again."

Nevertheless I wasn't so depressed or confused that we failed to go back to bed again together, and I felt warm and comforted in Charles' arms, as he explored my body. I stopped any argument or discussion. In his arms I had learnt at last to 'button my lip' and not always seek to have the last word. Yes, yes I was in love.

The next day when I got home in the afternoon Conradin was already there discussing the interminable 'ifs and buts' of June/July 1914 with Conrad. Of course I said nothing about what Charles had told me, but I did prick up my ears when I heard Conrad say to Conradin –

"Look, Conradin, the assassination in Sarajevo was the vital, the seminal event that set it all off. Yes of course there were underlying causes that led to war – though quite a few of these were closer to resolution than they had ever been before. Certainly, if there had never been a successful assassination, a European war could have broken out over some other incident. But it wouldn't have been the same war. Nothing is inevitable in History. Anything could have happened. The old Emperor would have died and Franz Ferdinand might have come to the throne. Anything could then have happened. The assassination was the vital act – the most seminal event in the whole of the Twentieth Century."

"Well OK grandpa – don't get excited. I understand what you are saying and I will concentrate on that."

"Hey, Conradin, it's the 17th June today. In eleven days it will be 28th June the anniversary of the day of the assassination. Let's both go to Sarajevo for a few days – trace for ourselves the route of the doomed couple and the conspirators, and see for ourselves the background. Even if we don't get any great revelation as to what happened, it will give you a feel for the background that no amount of reading from books could provide."

Well I could see immediately that Conradin was fascinated by the idea. Conrad said that he would clear it with William – after all what better person could there be with whom to explore the Bosnian capital than Conrad who had been there so often whilst covering the break-up of Yugoslavia.

I listened to all this, but I didn't think at all of the fact that I had just been told that the CPS was going to prosecute. Instead I worried about the danger. I pointed out that the war had only ended a year or so ago. Wasn't the Balkans the place where everyone hated each other and went round committing atrocities against each other left right and centre. I tentatively raised this point when I finally managed to intervene and get the attention of the two overgrown schoolboys who were excitedly making plans. Conrad completely pooh-poohed the idea of any danger whatsoever from the people of Sarajevo whom he had come to like and admire so much. He said that at no time had he felt any personal danger throughout his experience covering the wars. I remained unsure of the wisdom of the plan – but then I was only Conradin's aunt – it would be up to William to decide. Oddly enough at no time did it cross my mind that the CPS, having decided to prosecute, the Police might prevent Conrad from going abroad anywhere.

In the end it was of course not my problem. Two days later I heard my father organising a flight to Zagreb and realised that my brother William had agreed to the proposed trip. Three more days later, Charles took me out and then in the warm intimacy of his flat he asked me to marry him. I ecstatically accepted him and we made love. It was the 22nd June and Nikko organised a wonderful family party the very next day in celebration of my news. Everyone was there and Nikko surpassed himself with the delicious food he prepared. Conrad and Conradin flew off the next day which was the 24th June.

Chapter 28

Rasimir

I wandered the streets of Belgrade for days after the end of the NATO bombing campaign, passing and re-passing the ruined house which I had shared with my mother. I can see my mother – I can really see her right now – she is the Goddess Isis and she is standing right by me and stretches her hand out to me. I wander around without any idea what I am eating or what I am doing. One day I slip and fall in the street and fall fast asleep. Can this be a hospital? Everybody is so busy – so busy. I am given all sorts of pills to swallow and yes for a time I see everything a little more focussed.

The doctor is right. Now that my mother is dead, I will go back to Sarajevo where I am sure I still have friends who will remember me. I have some money but I don't know where it came from. I keep having nightmares. I relive my mother's screams every night. I decide when I leave the hospital that I may be able to clear the fuzziness in my mind by walking to Sarajevo. No train, no buses – I'll just walk and clear my mind as I go.

Frontier? What frontier. Don't we all live in one country!

No – it seems we don't anymore, and it is that and the bombs that has changed my life and cost me both my parents. As I walked through the countryside, although I became physically fitter, the continual pounding thoughts in my head would not go away. I found myself dwelling on subjects which I had never dreamed of before. Was I 17 or 18 – it was all so misty. Wild thoughts run through my head, which I knew if I ever mentioned them to anyone I would have been told that

I was being unreasonable. Was I losing my mind? I walked from village to village, past ruins and through towns still with ugly bomb damage. I slept in barns and on hayricks. Kind people gave me food sometimes. Why did they shake their heads at me as if they were sorry about something that they saw in my eyes?

Isis was instructing me that I needed to make a sacrifice. Only by a ritual act of killing and bloodshed could I be free of what was tearing me apart. It didn't need to be an act of revenge striking at a whole nation or a whole culture. I was simply required to find and make a sacrifice of one significant person who could represent it all in himself – or indeed in herself, why not - the whole culture which had turned my country into a desert, bombed its people and left me in this state of complete uncertainty as to who I was and what I was doing.

Voices are continually telling me that I would not achieve inner peace until I had arranged this sacrifice. It was clear to me that I was being called upon by divine forces – Isis and Osiris - to do battle with the Devil. That is to say the Devil that was in me, and the Devil that was out there. But who was it to be, where was I going to find the man or woman who would have to be sacrificed in order to redeem all the harm that had been done to me, my family, my people, and my country. I walked on and at last got to Sarajevo. It is no use asking me what day it was – I had lost track of all time – but it was certainly at the start of summer as I was no longer cold and the bombing had long since finished. Wait – I do recall the millennium celebrations taking place earlier so it was certainly after that bit of foolishness.

I settled in, in Sarajevo, in a basement room that I found – but I found no friends. Those I had known while my Dad was alive had either all died or had moved. To be honest I did not try very hard – after all I had the comfort of my voices. I managed to get a humble job with the municipality as a street cleaner. There weren't that many of us, as the Town Hall could not afford a proper full complement even at the poor rate we were being paid. On top of the pressure from Isis, I was being watched all the time by someone who was trying to injure my health. I don't know who it was – I never managed to catch him, but he was there somewhere watching all the time ready to pounce if I ever relaxed my guard.

After a few weeks I came to realise – as Isis explained it to me – that I did not need to find a statesman or a great figure from those countries who bombed us. I needed only to sacrifice someone who would be a symbol - that was all that was needed – a symbol of the hated people who had bombed us out of existence. Bombed us, so they said, entirely for our own good. Can you believe it? I had to lie pinned down in a ruined building with my own mother alongside, and hear her screams as she died a long and painful death. Then I had to lie alongside her dead body without being able to hold her hand – and why – why - because some people I have never seen, people whose actions I would have deplored if I had known anything about it, were supposedly killing other people in a province far from where I myself and my mother lived. These smug westerners, it seems, were upset about it. So they bombed us. Who cares whether they didn't mean to kill innocent residents – that is what they did. Then a few months later, after all our lives were ruined they turned to something else that pricked their delicate conscience.

I hate them all, and my voices are quite clear. I was called upon to act. A blood sacrifice to resolve the matter!

Bit by bit I began coming out of the daze in which I

had been living. I had been given a purpose - my mother Isis was directing me and I began looking around me much more. I suddenly realised that I was in fact surrounded by these smug westerners – soldiers from all sorts of countries were swaggering around, in our cafes and striding down our streets as if they owned them – which I suppose they did.. They weren't actually doing much so far as I could see – just being there. However, somehow, killing a random soldier was not quite the sacrifice that my voices were urging on me. I wanted something or someone that would make a greater impact and draw attention to the wrong done to us. A soldier, after all, puts his life on the line – and if one of them died it would make no impact. If I couldn't kill an Archduke, or a President or some so-called statesman, I would kill a total innocent. Somebody preferably young, someone whose life in the prosperous country he came from was full of promise and ready to be enjoyed. Someone as innocent as me!

I began manoeuvring to take the street cleaning rounds near the centre of the town, watching the comings and goings of the Western tourists who were just beginning to drift back, to watch us in our ruined condition, and to take photos of our picturesque misery.

No one ever quite seemed to fit the bill – but then one day I saw him. He was about my age – clean and cheerful and full of a life which for him was going to be free of dirt and squalor, and was going to be very fulfilling. He was wearing a white T shirt with a British Union Jack logo on the right shoulder.. He had on his head an American style baseball cap to shield his eyes from our strong Balkan sun. As if to make certain that he was the right one, in a band round the rim of the cap was the US Stars and Stripes. I couldn't have found a better representative of all that was eating me up. My voices were unambiguous – they called out 'surely this is your ideal sacrificial subject'. My anxieties and the pressures in my mind rolled away, and I became calm and clear in my resolve. I took the necessary first step and acquired a revolver.

Chapter 29

Sarajevo

Even in the year 2000 after most of the active trouble had ended, travel to the quasi-independent state of Bosnia-Herzegovina was not all that easy. But Conrad of course had contacts and ways and means arising from his work during the nineties as a journalist.

Conrad and his grandson arrived in Sarajevo on the 24th June. They settled in to their hotel, which was in the centre of town and took their first walk along the route taken by Franz Ferdinand and his wife when they first entered the city, almost a hundred years ago. It was a hot afternoon and both of them were in shirtsleeves. Conradin was wearing a white Tshirt with a prominent Union Jack logo on his shoulder. His eyes had always been a bit sensitive to bright sunlight, but he had never liked dark glasses, so instead he also sported an American baseball cap with a wide brim which shielded his eyes. Conrad found it all a bit over the top particularly as the baseball cap also sported the Stars and Stripes – but the only comment he made was –

"Conrad, do you really want to look so much like a tourist?" To which he got the firm answer –

"Why not Grandpa – we are tourists after all aren't we," delivered with a cheeky grin. He was clearly already enjoying himself.

* * * * *

The Archduke Franz Ferdinand was a man of enormous contradictions. He was the nephew of the old Emperor Franz Joseph. He had become the heir apparent to the Hapsburg monarchy of Austria-Hungary as a result of the suicide of his cousin the Archduke Rudolph, the only son of the old Emperor. Franz Ferdinand was a man of extremes. He could only 'love' or 'hate' and his feelings always burst into excess. But he had clear ideas about how the ramshackle Empire he would inherit could be reformed when he came to the throne.. He championed the idea of a 'federal' solution to the multi-national Empire. How this could work out in practice was not of course easy. The Empire was now a Dual monarchy – a combination of German and Magyar shared power. Trialism or the inclusion of the South Slavs as a separate unit of the Empire, which he appeared to favour was all very well, but the Hungarians wanted nothing to do with it, as it would reduce their power and they disliked Franz Ferdinand as much as he disliked them. Furthermore there were other Slavs too – the sophisticated Czechs of Bohemia, and the Poles of Galicia just to name two of the many other nationalities within the Empirer. Virulent nationalism was all the rage throughout Europe and both the multi-national Ottoman and Hapsburg Empires were finding it difficult to adapt.

Once he became the Heir Apparent to the Empire his movements of course became more circumscribed. He was still in his twenties when it was noted that he had become a frequent visitor to the establishment of one of the Archduchesses of the Empire. It was rumoured and believed that he had fallen in love with her eldest daughter and would in due course ask for her hand in marriage. But then one day the Archduchess in question – Isabella - a stiff and superior grande dame found the photograph of one of her ladies-in-waiting – a certain Sophie Chotek - in a medallion belonging to Franz Ferdinand. Sophie was not a commoner – she was a

Countess in her own right – but she was not of royal stock. She was from an ancient but now impoverished Bohemian family. The haughty Archduchess, who had always imagined that the young Franz Ferdinand was interested in one of her eligible daughters, fired the beautiful young Sophie on the spot.

But Franz Ferdinand was deeply in love with Sophie and immediately proposed to her and asked Francis Joseph for permission to marry her. The court was scandalised and Francis Joseph wanted to refuse outright any permission to marry. This was nothing to do with the fact that Sophie was from a Czech family – it was simply the strict requirement that the heir apparent could only marry either another Hapsburg – or a member of one of the other European Royal Houses. But the young and stubborn Franz Ferdinand was adamant and persistent. Eventually with many people, including even the Pope, supporting him, the old Emperor, perhaps remembering his own son's suicide, finally relented and allowed the marriage, but only on condition that it was to be a morganatic marriage. Franz Ferdinand had to take a solemn oath in front of other members of the family and to sign a formal Deed accepting that his wife would not have Archduchess status and that none of his children could become Archdukes or have any claim to any succession. This Deed of Renunciation was signed by Franz Ferdinand on the 28th June 1900.

The 28th June!

This day was' Vidovdan' – one of the holiest days in the Serbian Orthodox calendar. St Vitus' day! But much more to the point it was also the day in 1389 when the Ottomans defeated the medieval Serbian Kingdom at the Battle of Kosovo, and took over Serbia which became part of their Empire for the next 400 years.. On the very same evening of that massive defeat, a Serbian

Knight who had survived the slaughter, entered the tent of the victorious Sultan – Murad I – and assassinated him. There was no Serbian teenager who did not know this story.

Franz Ferdinand was the senior Inspector-General of the Army, and he took his duties very seriously. A fairly large part of the Austro-Hungarian army was stationed in Bosnia. Sometime towards the end of 1913 Franz Ferdinand had been asked to attend the Imperial Army manoeuvres to be held in the following year in Bosnia. That was fine, but then it was decided, with a complete disregard for possible popular feelings, that after the exercise was complete, he should make an official visit to Sarajevo to give encouragement to those in the province – and there were many – who supported the monarchy. But the day chosen was the 28th June! It was as if, at the height of the Irish troubles also in the same year 1914, the British government had requested the Prince of Wales to make an official visit to Dublin, and had then chosen St. Patrick's Day as the day of the entry into the town.

Before he left for the manoeuvres and the official visit Franz Ferdinand was depressed and had a foreboding of possible trouble and seriously considered at least cancelling the visit if not the manoeuvres. But here a significant factor came into play. Due to the stuffy Viennese Court protocols and the refusal to accept Sophie as an Archduchess, he could rarely have Sophie by his side during his public appearances as a Hapsburg Prince. But in his capacity as Inspector-General of the Army, Sophie could be with him at his public appearances. It was this which caused him to override his anxiety about the visit.. He would go and he would take Sophie with him. By then they had three children – an eldest daughter Sophie who actually survived into the 1990's at the start of the break-up of Yugoslavia – and 2 sons Maximilian and Ernst who were 12 and 10 in 1914. It was always a very happy marriage with parents and children close to one another.

Franz Ferdinand arrived in Ilidze, a small health resort just north of Sarajevo, and Sophie joined him here on the 25th June. For two days he attended the Army manoeuvres and he even paid an incognito visit to Sarajevo. His friendly feelings towards the Slavs were known and accepted throughout Bosnia – though not of course in Serbia – and even the opposition press accorded him a welcome.

The morning of the 28th June was a radiant sunny Sunday. Franz Ferdinand and the beautiful Sophie first attended early morning Mass together, then left by train for Sarajevo to pay the long-planned official visit to the town.

* * * * *

Rasimir had no really clear definable national identity in Balkan terms. His father was a Croat, but one who had disapproved of Tudjman from the start. His mother was a Serb, but the vicissitudes of his life were such that he had never felt close to her until the very end. He had, however, enjoyed his visits to his mother's parents in Bosnia. He was undersized and frail-looking. He looked emaciated with sallow sharp features. His clear blue eyes were burning and piercing, but now that he had finally decided what he was going to do, they had lost that rather insane look which had troubled people, and they were now fairly serene, with nothing too criminal or insane in their expression.

He had stopped work and began carefully stalking Conradin as he and Conrad strolled through the streets visiting the town's attractions. It is impossible to analyse completely why he had picked on this particular representative of the Western European he had come to hate with such maniacal intensity. There was an aspect which arose from the fact that the young man looked as if he was the same age as himself. But the Tshirt and the baseball cap was clearly a key element of why Isis had chosen Conradin. Rasimir's sanity drifted in and out, but once he had taken the decision, he was ready to kill and to die if necessary. However, he had no idea what date it was at any time as he stalked the young man. He was not acting as a Serb. His insane hatred stemmed entirely from his personality – his past. It was what Razmik in Azerbaijan had specifically rejected, when he refused to end up hating all Azeris collectively. It was akin to the attitude of the crowd in a back-street of Calcutta who gathered when one of the children in the community was run over and killed by a municipal bus driver. The driver, who was undoubtedly driving too fast, did not stop but drove on to report at the next nearest police station, as advised by the Police and urged on by all the passengers in his bus, The crowd that had gathered, frustrated, waited and stopped the next municipal bus to come along – pulled out that driver and killed him. It was the same principle at work, but one which Razmik had deliberately rejected

* * * * *

On arrival at the station in Sarajevo, the Archduke's party was received by the Mayor together with other dignitaries of the town. They all went out to the four official cars which were parked outside and which were to take them to a formal reception at the Town Hall. In the first car was the Mayor himself together with the senior police officer. In the second car with it's canvas hood opened fully back was the Archduke in full dress uniform and beside him in the back seat was his beloved wife Sophie enjoying the rare pleasure of being with her husband on a grand formal occasion, and in such wonderful weather too. Facing them sitting back to the front of the car was General Potiorek, the Imperial Governor of Bosnia. Sitting next to the chauffeur at the front was a local Count – Count Harrach – who was the owner of this grand made-to–order 'Graf und Stift' motorcar, beautifully handcrafted, made in Vienna in 1910. He had leant it to the town for the use of the Archduke on his official visit.

To get to the Town Hall the cars had first to reach the Appel Quay which went alongside the River Miljacka, always almost dried up in summer. This road was bordered on one side by a line of houses – on the other by a low wall below which flowed, or rather usually flowed, the River. There were on that day six conspirators who had slipped across the frontier from Serbia a day or two before. They were Bosnian Serbs – that is to say citizens of the Austro-Hungarian Empire not citizens of Serbia. All six had positioned themselves along the Quay – the Archduke's itinerary and route had been openly published. Near the Cumuria bridge, the first bridge to be passed by the motorcade, were 3 of the conspirators in a line on the riverside. On the landward side further on, stood another. On the riverside at the next bridge – the Lateiner bridge - stood Gavrilo Princip on his own. Finally at the third bridge there was one more. All six of them were each armed with a bomb and each had a small revolver as well, all provided by …….. well, even now, that is so controversial a subject as to require many pages of text. But there is no controversy as to the numbers – there were six of them!! Such an extraordinary range of conspirators drew the remark from the Archbishop of Sarajevo that it would have been a miracle if the Archduke had left the city alive. But as it happened the assassins – almost all of them below the age of 21 and mostly just teenagers – were so inefficient that it was a singular series of chances that he was harmed at all.

As the motorcade passed, the first two assassins standing on the riverside of the road didn't do anything at all. The third assassin – Cabrinovic – detonated his bomb by striking it against the lamppost he had been leaning against and then threw it at the Archduke seated at the back of the open car. But he threw just that bit too far and the bomb landed on the hood that was folded right back and it then bounced off onto the road behind and exploded under the front of the next car behind, injuring one of the officers in that car. Meanwhile, Cabrinovic, after failing to poison himself, the cyanide pill he had been given didn't work, jumped into the bed of the River below, where he was pursued and caught by the police. After ascertaining what had happened, Franz Ferdinand ordered the procession, now reduced to three cars, to proceed to the Town Hall.

* * * * *

It was the 28th June – Vidovdan. Trying accurately to retrace the route taken by the Imperial couple, Conrad and Conradin reached the site of what was previously known as the Cumuria Bridge. Here they stopped and considered what had happened here all those years ago. Conradin looked over the low embankment wall at the river below – it had been a wet spring and there was a good deal more water in it than when Cabrinovic had jumped. Conradin remarked at how high it was and how it was that Cabrinovic in such a tense moment had not only jumped but had managed to land safely and to stagger away before he was caught.. But Conrad who seemed distracted said only –

"He was fit enough – don't forget they were all only kids. Cabrinovic was I think still only a teenager."

They strolled on towards the old Town Hall – but it became clear to Conradin that his grandfather was distracted by something.

It was not for nothing that Conrad had been an Intelligence Officer with the Army for 7 years. Not for nothing that he had been dropped behind enemy lines twice and had spied for the Eighth Army in Nazi-occupied Rome for almost a whole year. His experiences had given him a sixth sense often attained by such agents. A sense of impending danger! He began to feel that someone was following them. Once he accepted that thought as they strolled down the Appel Quay, he suddenly became convinced that they had also been followed the previous day. His first thought, natural to a journalist of his type, was that it must be some secret government police – for in his experience danger came not from criminals but from the authorities.

He kept looking round but at no time did he see anything or anyone acting suspiciously. He couldn't rid himself of the feeling, but it was a lovely day and he was enjoying it all so much that he wasn't going to spoil it and instinct could also let you down. So they strolled on and when they reached the Lateiner bridge they both agreed that it was time for a spot of lunch. They found a small restaurant – not much more than a café really, near the bridge and went in for the rather sparse food that was on offer.

Meanwhile Rasimir had been keeping them both in his sights from the moment that they had emerged from the hotel. He may have still been in a daze as to what he was actually eventually going to do, but his senses were as alert as they had ever been, and he immediately noticed that the older man – surely too old just to be the boy's father – seemed to have become aware that they were being followed and was looking round. Rasimir felt the comforting grip of the revolver in his pocket – but then took immediate steps to walk away. He went well away as the pair dallied at the Cumuria bridge. He knew nothing whatsoever about the events of the 28th June in 1914, but it was fairly obvious that the two tourists were going to carry on strolling up the quayside – and so it was.

By the time Conrad and Conradin entered the little restaurant on the other side of the road Rasimir himself was fairly hungry – but he had gone without food so often that he had no difficulty in making do with a coffee in another café which didn't serve food on the same corner, but across the road. He watched the door across the road as he waited for the couple to finish their lunch. He still had no real idea how he was going to effect the death that he was determined upon. He was not practised in the art of shooting. He knew that he couldn't simply walk into the restaurant opposite, walk past all the other tables, and then be sure to shoot the boy and the boy alone in that smoke-filled and noisy environment. It was clear that he would have to wait for the tourists to come out and this time he would be prepared. He was already sitting by the door. He ordered a second coffee, paid his Bill and waited.

* * * * *

At the Town Hall the flustered Mayor began to read his speech of welcome. However, before he had got much further than the first florid opening, Franz Ferdinand interrupted him and said –

"Mr. Mayor I came here on a friendly visit and I get bombs thrown at me. I find it outrageous – but please now proceed."

As the Reception proceeded, Franz Ferdinand now discussed the situation with Potiorek and asked him whether he thought there would be any more bombs. The General, who, considering the provocative circumstances, had in fact been lax about the security aspects of the visit, replied that he did not think so. However, just in case, he suggested that it might be better to change the Schedule planned for the rest of the day. Instead of going to visit the Museum in the old town which was the next item on the official agenda – they should drive back fast along the Appel Quay and either drive all the way straight back to Ilidze, or go to the station and take the train. But by then Franz Ferdinand had been told that the officer in the third car had been taken to the hospital, and he insisted that it was his duty to pay him a visit and make sure he was all right. In any event after some discussion, that was the route finally agreed. They would drive back down the Appel Quay as fast as possible and then go on to the hospital. The original schedule which was to go back as far as the Lateiner Bridge then turn right and go up the narrow Franz Joseph street to the Museum was abandoned.

Sophie, who was originally required to go directly to the Governor's residence for a small reception there with some of the ladies of the town, decided instead to accompany her husband, and again took her seat beside him. As they all got back into the cars, this time Potiorek was in the front next to the driver, and the young Count Harrach stood on the running board on the left-hand side – that is to say the river side - from which side

Cabrinovic had thrown his bomb, and indeed the side on which all the conspirators had been standing. The idea was that he could shield the couple with his body in case there were any conspirators left.

Meanwhile Princip had heard the sound of the bomb. He strolled back following the crowd in that direction and saw that the procession was at a standstill. His first thought was that the attempt had been successful and he saw Cabrinovic being taken away by the police from the riverbed. But then he saw the procession setting off again and he realised that the attempt had failed. He believed that the afternoon schedule required the cars to turn right into Franz Joseph Street, so somewhat fortuitously he strolled across to take up a position on the other, the town side of the Quay.

* * * * *

It was odd that during the long lunch that Conrad and Conradin had together in the corner café, Conrad became more anxious. As he thought back to earlier in the day, whilst half listening to Conradin's joyful enthusiasms, he was now quite sure that they had been followed. He knew that he could usually recognise a policeman, secret or not, at any distance, but he had not spotted anyone who would have fitted. Meanwhile, Conradin was keen to clear up all their thoughts and discussions on the historical consequences of the assassination. He was enjoying the whole atmosphere, together with being in such a close relationship with his grandfather. Conrad cleared his mind shook his head, tried to forget his apprehension and paid more attention to what Conradin was saying –

"It's all very well Grandpa, but I've read that many historians and commentators have said that this event was simply a trigger, and that the situation in Europe was such that some war was going to break out somewhere – and that if it didn't arise from the events of the 28th June, it would have started on some other incident later."

"I don't agree, Conradin. Many of the so-called underlying tensions and causes for conflict were in the course of being settled. Anglo-German Naval rivalry, always thought of as an important underlying cause, was in the course of being resolved. The Berlin to Baghdad railway was no longer contentious. France was in no state to start anything. As I said before, Conradin, anything could have happened. The old Emperor would certainly have died and the whole situation in the Austro-Hungarian Empire would have changed on the accession of Franz Ferdinand. It was the instability of the Vienna regime that was the whole cause of European instability and who can say what might have happened on the change of the monarchs. Above all, in answer to all those who say that any little incident might have set off the war, you must remember that much the same rulers, much the same foreign ministers, Ambassadors and Generals, had all been in place for the previous ten years, when there had been a spate of incidents and crises – all of which had been dealt with and any war averted by patient diplomacy. But this particular incident was not just another trigger. It could not be resolved and it led directly to the Great War and the end of old Europe."

On the other corner of the street, Rasimir was getting impatient. He knew what he was going to do, he simply wasn't sure how he was going to do it. He knew he could not simply walk into the opposite café and gun down the young man. He may have been approaching complete insanity, but he was still aware of his limitations. He would stumble in there, he would miss and the whole thing would be a shambles. But did he have the nerve to wait inactive like this. Sitting there was torture. He had had enough – it would have to be another day. He got up, nodded at the waiter and walked out. Whatever it was he wanted to do it would not be today.

* * * * *

Potiorek's plan had been accepted. The couple were duly seated at the back of the open-topped car, with Count Harrach on the running board on the left hand side. But Potiorek and the Police Chief, neither of whom really believed that there could be a second attempt, not only failed to realise the possible danger of driving back along any part of the Appel Quay, but above all also failed to give clear instructions to the two chauffeurs.

What then happened was a whole extraordinary series of accidents and coincidences that no one, least of all any of the conspirators, could have predicted. There were now two cars in the procession. The cars drove along the Appel Quay at some speed as arranged. There was no way anyone could have fired successfully at any of the occupants. But then the chauffeur of the front car, not having been properly instructed, turned right at the Lateiner Bridge and into the narrow Franz Joseph Street heading for the museum. The Archduke's car, immediately behind, naturally followed suit. Potiorek excitedly ordered the driver to stop and back out, back onto the Appel Quay to continue as agreed. The car stopped and was slowly beginning to back out – and there standing on the corner, on the right hand side of the now almost stationery car stood Gavrilo Princip, who had almost without thinking strolled across earlier.

Even at that stage if the car had simply followed

the other nothing could have happened. But with the car slowly beginning to back out into the Appel Quay and almost stationery, only a few paces away from the amazed Princip, he found himself staring straight at the imperial couple. Hemmed in by crowds cheering, he could not throw his bomb. Instead he shut his eyes – or so he said afterwards - and fired two shots. He could only fire the two before the crowd was on to him before he could kill himself with another bullet, which was his intention.

The first shot hit the Archduke in the jugular vein – the second wounded Sophie in the abdomen. Sophie, who didn't at first seem to realise that she too had been shot, cried out as she saw the blood on Franz Ferdinand's lips –

"For God's sake what has happened to you"

She then sank down and ended up with her head on her husband's lap. She was already dead, but the Archduke didn't realise – nor did Count Harrach who thought she had just fainted.

The Archduke now repeated several times getting fainter all the time –

"Ah Sophie…Sophie .. don't die – live – live – for our children.. Ah my children,..Sophie..Sophie."

The car, now back on the Quayside and facing the right direction sped on – but when they arrived at the governor's residence, Sophie was long since dead. Franz Ferdinand died about ten minutes after his body was taken into the building.

Despite every effort by all those same foreign ministers, ambassadors, chancellors, Kings and Princes, the European Powers, neither the selfish nation-states nor the declining multi-national empires could avoid the cataclysm. One month after the assassination, mobilizations had already begun and on the 1st August, European War began – a war which was joined by the British Empire on the 4th, and by the Ottoman Empire a few weeks later.

* * * * *

Conrad and his grandson at last finished their second cup of coffee. Conradin who had actually been taking notes as his grandfather went on and on about the way in which the Europeans had from the 28th June onwards drifted into a war which certainly none of the civilian leaders wanted. He grinned as he closed his notebook and said –

"Grandpa – I've really enjoyed these three days. Thank you. I shall remember them for the rest of my life."

"Come, come" said Conrad somewhat embarrassed by the intensity of Conradin's words and body language. "I've enjoyed them too – it's rounded off all my own thoughts and experiences about the Balkans and what happened with the demise of the Ottoman and Hapsburg Empires."

"Back to London and the grind early tomorrow morning", said Conradin and got up. Conrad had already paid, and he too rose, though neither as quickly or as easily as the teenager.

Conradin got to the door of the restaurant and walked out into the sunshine, putting on his baseball cap, just as Rasimir appeared at the door of the café on the other side of the street, with a view to giving up and going home. It was once again a confrontation that was entirely fortuitous and would have been avoided if Conradin had sat on for only a further two or three minutes. Rasimir stared across at the youth standing quite still on the pavement right opposite him, waiting for his grandfather to join him. He was a perfect target. But Rasimir was not any kind of trained assassin – basically he was as amateur and inefficient as all the other assassins who had been on this Quayside on the same day all those years ago. He hesitated and then felt for his revolver, pulling it somewhat clumsily out of his baggy trousers – then raising it and taking some sort of aim.

It was at that moment, as it came out of his pocket, that Conrad himself emerged from the restaurant and onto the pavement. He would probably have been too late to react, if it had not been for the fact that he was already alert for some sort of danger. He saw the man on the other side of the street – he saw the revolver coming out of the pocket – and he saw that the man's insane eyes were trained directly on Conradin. He was seventy-seven, but he had not forgotten all those years in the field. In the end it is the 'will' that counts as it overcomes the feebleness of the body. He sprang forward and in a clumsy rugby tackle he brought Conradin's body crashing to the ground, just before a first shot rang out.

Rasimir had no idea what had happened. He too had closed his eyes as he fired. He simply saw that the old man had fallen down on top of his intended victim. He also saw that the old man was now scrambling up and coming straight across the road at him. Without thinking he acted blindly again, firing a second shot at the oncoming figure. This second bullet hit Conrad directly in the chest, but this was not a massive firearm, it had not stopped Conrad's onward rush, and his body smashed into Rasimir and brought him crashing down to the ground with his revolver pinned so that he was unable to fire anything again.

By now enough bystanders had been alerted to the situation and the traffic had stopped. A policeman was already running up from further down the Quay. Conradin had been winded by the fall, but found his feet quickly and ran across the street, where two men already had Rasimir held tightly and had taken away his gun. But Conrad, bleeding badly from his chest could not move and his eyes were closed. Conradin bent down and with his tears now flowing, whispered into Conrad's ear –

"It's me Grandpa – it's me – please say something – please please.. "

Conradin knelt down and cradled his grandfather in his arms, willing him to open his eyes and acknowledge him. Slowly Conrad's eyes did open, but even at only 17 years old, Conradin could see that the old man did not recognise him.

Then Conrad's eyes lit up for a brief moment as he focused on Conradin bending over him –

"Billy?" he said – and died.

www.ingramcontent.com/pod-product-compliance
Lightning Source LLC
Chambersburg PA
CBHW030329030726
47499CB00003B/693